SLUDGE-GULPERS

Jane Waller was born in Aylesbury, Buckinghamshire and brought up in Oxfordshire. She has a BA in Sculpture as well as an MA in Ceramics from the Royal College of Art. She has written copiously on subjects as wide ranging as ceramics and fashion, and her first published children's novel, *Below the Green Pond*, was voted among the Pick of the Year by the Federation of Children's Book Clubs. Her second children's novel, *Saving the Dinosaurs*, is published by Macmillan Children's Books. She lives with her husband in London by the river Thames, but writes in a cottage in the Chilterns.

Also by Jane Waller

Saving the Dinosaurs

JANE WALLER

Sludge-Gulpers

For Natalie,
with best wishes
from the author,
Jane Waller

MACMILLAN
CHILDREN'S BOOKS

First published 1997 by Macmillan Children's Books

a division of Macmillan Publishers Limited
25 Eccleston Place, London SW1W 9NF
and Basingstoke

Associated companies throughout the world

ISBN 0 330 34428 5

1 3 5 7 9 8 6 4 2

A CIP catalogue record for this book is available from
the British Library

Phototypeset by Intype London Ltd
Printed by Mackays of Chatham PLC, Chatham, Kent

Before the London sewers were built, sewage used to be carried along in open ditches. The Fleet Ditch was one of them.

The Open Fleet Ditch

'Filth of all hues and odours seem to tell
What street they sailed from, by their sight and smell . . .
Sweepings from butchers' stalls, dung, guts, and blood,
Drowned puppies, stinking sprats, all drenched in mud,
Dead cats and turnip tops came tumbling down the flood . . .'

Jonathan Swift

'Your Fleet Lane Furies and hot cooks do dwell
That with still scalding streams make the place hell;
The sinks run grease, and hair of meazled hogs
The heads, houghs, entrails, and the hide of dogs.'

Ben Johnson

It was not until the 'Great Stink' of 1858 (when the windows of the Houses of Parliament had to be draped with curtains soaked in chloride of lime so that members could breathe), that an act was passed resulting in Joseph Bazalgette's plan to improve the sewers. Three large new sewers running north of the Thames and two on the south crossed London from west to east, intercepting the old sewers on the way to the embankment.

Nowadays, sewage is treated by a method named the 'activated sludge process', and the residue is carried by special ships called 'gravy boats' sixty miles out to the North Sea, where it is dumped. In spite of all the dangers, the health of the sewermen (or 'Flushers') does not suffer, and they do not seem to mind the conditions in which they work.

Note

I have changed the names of a few of the London Sewers I have used – some have rather weighty names like 'The Ranelagh and King's Scholars Pond Relief Sewer'. Some of the sewers have been moved to fit the plot.

Bibliography
London under London Trench and Hillman (pub. 1984)
Underground London Hollingshead (pub. 1861)
Mayhew's London (first pub. 1851)
The Lost Rivers of London Nicholas Barton (pub. 1962)

To Michael

Acknowledgements

Chiefly to my editor, Marion Lloyd ... for keeping me at it.

Also for their help and encouragement: Chris and Clare Griffin, Lyn and David Griffin, Steve McCabe, and my husband, Michael.

To Chris Foreman, Alan Lenander and all the Flushers at Hammersmith MD Depot, for allowing me to go down under London. And to the Brighton Flushers in the Southern Water Services Ltd. Sussex Division, for a tour of the Brighton Sewers.

Contents

CHAPTER ONE

The Service Lift

When Suzie stepped into the street after school was over, she found London completely changed. The atmosphere was so tense that it prickled her skin, rather like air charged with electricity before a storm. Walking home with Clare and Jane today was incredibly difficult. In Buckingham Palace Road they had to keep pushing through clusters of people who had poured into the street to hear the extraordinary news.

'*Abdication special!*' the newspaper-seller shouted.

'ROYAL FAMILY ENDS AFTER A THOUSAND YEARS OF RULE! REFERENDUM RESULT SHOCK: COUNTRY VOTES FOR A REPUBLIC – HER MAJESTY TO RETIRE!' were headlines that screamed from every paper.

'So, it's actually happening. How exciting!'

1

cried Clare. 'My mother definitely voted for a Republic.'

'Well, my mother didn't,' said Jane. 'She wouldn't dream of getting rid of the Monarchy. And it isn't exciting at all. I think it's terrible. You know what a Republic will mean. Just a prime minister in charge of the country – no Royalty at all. It's bound to be extremely boring.'

And they began to argue like everybody else. The referendum, in which the people had to vote for keeping the Monarchy or for becoming a Republic, was a close-run thing. The voting margin had been narrow. Now the people were divided.

As the three girls turned into Sutherland Street, Suzie dropped behind a little to be on her own. She found it difficult to concentrate on what was happening to the country when there was so much going on inside her own head to deal with. Ever since Dad had decided to leave home to be with Victoria Snaresbrook, she and Mum had been on their own. Now all her thoughts and feelings had tied themselves into a hard knot somewhere inside her brain. It was almost as if her head didn't belong to her any more, as if her mind had been wrapped in a tight parcel – not to be undone until Dad came back. But deep down, she knew this would never happen. The old life had gone for ever.

Once they had lived in a whole house with a large garden. But without Dad, their old home had to be sold, and Mrs Stanmore found a job hand-painting flower designs on to china tea-sets and mugs. Suzie and her mother moved into a high-rise block in Pimlico so that her mother didn't have so far to travel. Their new flat was miles up on the eighteenth floor. In this smaller place there was nowhere to play, and no one to play with. Monument, her very own black kitten, had had to be given away.

Suzie could see their block in the distance, a remote slab pressing darkly into the sky.

They had just passed Sussex Street when Suzie stopped short and clutched the bus stop for support. Her heart was beating suddenly very fast. Her throat felt as if it had been squeezed.

'I can't be dreaming it this time,' she reasoned. 'Exactly the same thing happened yesterday . . . and the day before.'

There, right in the middle of the road, the heavy manhole cover twitched, lifted itself up – huge, sad eyes peered out – and two slimy fingers beckoned, trying to draw her close.

'Come over here,' they seemed to plead.

'I must be going mad,' she thought, wildly.

'Hurry up, Suzie! What's wrong?'

'Nothing,' she called, trying not to make her voice tremble. She walked quickly on, but with

3

a nasty sensation in the small of her back, as if someone was following her . . .

Suzie waved goodbye to Clare, who turned off into her road. Walking with Clare was the best part of the journey home. Clare usually had something to chatter about, and was always full of fun. Suzie knew she hadn't been much company for her best friend lately. But Clare understood. Jane was different, she often whined and was irritating. She was only really interested in herself. *Her* opinion was always right. But Suzie could hardly not walk home with Jane – seeing that they both lived in the same block.

When Suzie opened the door of their flat, the television was blaring out the latest on the Queen's retirement.

'It has been announced that the Abdication Ceremony is to be a Coronation-in-reverse. Her Majesty will arrive at Westminster Abbey in her state coach. She will process along the nave to sit on the throne for the last time. There, her crown will be ceremonially removed and she will give up her sceptre and orb, the ancient symbols of royal power.'

'Hello, darling,' Mrs Stanmore called. 'Isn't the news amazing? Do you realize that this is going to be a Major Moment of History? After

4

all the debate there's been, I can hardly believe we're actually going to get rid of the Royal Family – even though I did vote against them.'

Mrs Stanmore gave her daughter a hug and they both sat down to watch the rest of the news. The Queen had announced that she would like her abdication to take place as quickly as possible, and the following Friday had been decided on.

'It's good news for the firm,' said Mrs Stanmore. 'They're rushing out thousands of Abdication mugs and everyone has been transferred to painting them. We've all been asked to work overtime every evening, starting tonight.'

'Oh, Mum, I'll hardly ever see you.'

'I'll get an hour off before the evening shift every day – I'll prepare something nice for your supper, and you can do your homework and watch the telly.'

Suzie scowled.

'It's only for a week,' Mrs Stanmore went on. 'We really do need the extra money, now that Daddy ... And after the Abdication, there's going to be a spectacular firework display and laser show in Hyde Park. We'll go and have a fantastic time.'

She put on her coat.

'Your supper's ready to heat in the microwave

whenever you want. Now I really must be off, or I'll be late. Bye, darling.'

No sooner had the door slammed shut, than boredom fell like a stifling blanket over Suzie's head. She went over to the window and pressed her pale face against the cold glass, trying to trace with sharp blue eyes the speck that was her mother, as it disappeared into the grey smudge of London far below. Jane was right for once. Without a Monarchy, England would become as sad and bored as Suzie already felt.

'Well, here I am, left on my own, shut up high in the sky.' Suzie fiercely polished away the mist on the glass made from her breath, but the view of her mother had become distorted. She sighed, and left the window to tackle her homework.

'I suppose I'd better do the worst part first – maths.'

She opened her exercise book and, sweeping a bunch of floppy hair out of the way, glared at question 7: '$x = y+z$.' She chewed the end of her biro. 'That looks impossible. It is impossible! But if I don't try it, Mr Morden will go mad again. I suppose I'll have to bribe Jane to help.'

Suzie despised herself for asking favours from Jane, but Jane was a whizz at maths, and it only meant going to her flat on the ground floor. Suzie got the kitchen steps and climbed to the Smarties hidden on top of the saucepan cupboard. There was only one tube left.

'She usually demands two for a page of maths. Well, I'll try with one.'

She found her front door key and made for the lift. But when she reached it she stared at the notice.

'What *terrible* handwriting. It's worse than mine.'

The message was scrawled across a filthy piece of paper pinned to the door. The service lift was right at the other end of the corridor. It was a large, gloomy metal box, painfully slow. Suzie pressed the button. When the lift eventually arrived, she opened the heavy door-grating, got in, and slid it closed with a clunk, nearly crushing the Smarties and her maths.

She peered through the grating at every floor as it shivered past. On each landing there was a black door with a brass number in the middle, and a fitted doormat in front. The same scene rattled by, floor after floor, with only the odd empty milk bottle to vary the view. Then, after the ground floor slid from view, to Suzie's horror the heavy lift didn't stop. Instead, it went on trundling down and down and down . . .

'Help! What's happening? Where am I going . . .?'

CHAPTER TWO

Under London

C lunk! The lift ground to a halt. Suzie pushed the button to go up. Nothing happened. She pressed all the buttons. The door slid slowly open. Facing her was a ragged opening where bricks had been removed from the middle of a wall, as if a giant had pushed his fist through. Next to it was another notice, rather moist and fixed into place with what looked like a handful of sludge.

Suzie stared at the disgusting notice and then at the dark hole. She had become aware of a most extraordinary gurgling coming from the other

9

side, rather like bathwater going down the plug. She decided to peer through.

'What a weird place! And what a horrible *smell . . . ell . . . ell . . . ell . . . ell!*' her voice echoed back.

She saw a damp chamber with a low-arched, brick-built roof. From the ceiling, drops of water plopped heavily to the ground. The scene was lit by a glimmering light which filtered through a grating high above and speckled patterns over the sodden floor.

'Wow! This must be somewhere right under the edge of our building, and that light must come from the road.'

Putting her Smarties in her jacket pocket and tucking her maths under one arm, she decided to follow the mysterious instructions and explore. Bravely she climbed through the hole's darkness. Everything was so slippery, she'd have to be careful. But that's what Suzie's slim figure was best at: balancing, whirling on roller skates, scaling the climbing frames at school. As her eyes grew used to the gloom, she saw where the rushing noise was coming from.

There, running right along the end of the chamber, was a large, dark tunnel. It carried a slurry of grey watery sludge along its centre. Suzie was gazing at this in astonishment, when, in a rush of foul air, a large toad-like creature leapt suddenly from a shelf over her head and landed, *splat*, at her feet.

'*Ooaagh!*' she screamed.

The 'thing' – whatever it might be – was round, brown, slimy, and as high as her waist. It squatted in front of her, glistening with wetness from its finely webbed fingertips to its flatly webbed feet.

Petrified, Suzie clutched her maths book tight, while the revolting creature, its whole skin alive with blotches, stretched on sinewy legs to make an exaggerated bow.

'So pleased you could come,' it croaked. 'I didn't mean to scare you. I've been waiting for you for ages.' The rubbery lips on its bulbous face stretched in a hideous smile of welcome.

Suzie shook with fear. She turned to run back through the hole, but a wet, rubbery hand plucked at her sleeve so that she had to wriggle round to pull free.

'Please don't leave!' the creature implored. 'You've no idea the courage it took to get you down.'

And it was only then, seeing the smile cease and the large face grow sad and pleading, that Suzie recognized the creature to be the same that she had glimpsed pushing up the manhole cover in Sutherland Street. Then everything began to fall into place. The lift going wrong, the strange notes. Suzie realized she'd been successfully and skilfully tricked. She dashed for the lift but the sewer toad surged after her.

'Stop! Don't desert us! We've been trying so hard to get you here.'

'What do you mean *we?*' Suzie shot round, expecting a whole hoard of slimy creatures to appear.

'By my Foot in the Sludge!' it despaired. 'I wouldn't have dared bring you down if it wasn't of National Importance. We really do need your help.'

The creature looked very sorry for itself. Tears trembled from the rims of its bulging eyes.

'I – I can't help you this evening,' Suzie stammered. 'I've got homework to do. You don't know what Mr Morden is like. He'll kill me if I don't at least try to do it.'

'Killing you is a little extreme, isn't it? Homework doesn't sound much fun. Perhaps I can do it?' A gleam of hope replaced the tears.

'You? It's maths! Far too difficult for anyone, except Jane.'

'Maths presents no problems. I'm brilliant at mathematics, algebra, logic – all those kind of things.' A slimy hand reached eagerly for the book. 'Let me help. It's only writing I can't do – as you noticed.'

12

'So it *was* you who wrote those messages. Your handwriting's terrible.'

'I know, but I had to do something drastic. The other lift works perfectly,' the creature chuckled. 'You have to admit, it was a brilliant plan.'

'It was a horrible trick,' Suzie retorted. 'And it's cold and miserable down here. Where are we?'

'We're in the Main Sewers under London. All that stuff,' it indicated with a webbed hand, 'all that rushing along, is the waste from your houses. Of course it's relatively quiet at the moment, what with the fine weather Up Above. But when it pours, rainwater shoots along here from places as far as Highgate and Hampstead Heath. Sometimes this whole chamber fills to the brim. Although most sewer creatures swim well, the current grows fearfully strong.'

Suzie grew more and more uneasy; she hadn't learned to swim well enough to cope with a flood. Skidding around, she managed to dash for the lift, and drew the door-grating safely across. She pushed the button to go up. Nothing happened. Thoroughly alarmed, she pushed every button. All that happened was that the door started to open again.

'Oh no! Let me go up, please!' Helplessly she rattled the gate.

13

Seizing its chance, the sewer creature wedged a large foot in the gap. Then, flinging its arms wide in a desperate plea, implored, 'But we *chose* you. This was the only block in the whole area where I could make the lift go to the very bottom of the shaft. And *you* were the only person suitable in the whole building.'

Suzie, who had retreated to the far corner of the lift, considered this for a moment or two. No one had ever chosen her before – not for anything really important.

'But what about Jane? She's much more clever than me.'

'You are more special in every way. That other girl looks selfish and unfriendly. You've got guts, courage – just the kind of qualities we're looking for. We've observed you thoroughly.'

Suzie softened. Inside, she felt a glow of pride. It might be quite exciting to help these strange creatures that lived under London.

'I'm not brilliant at anything much, except gym – and I'm OK at English and art. But I'll help if I can. And if you do my maths.'

'Straight away. Straight away. Just give me the book.'

The foot was withdrawn. Tentatively, Suzie slid the door open. She wasn't sure she trusted this sewer-toad yet, but she held out her book.

Casually the creature thumbed through to the most recent page, then carried the book closer to the pool of flickering light.

'Hey, this is easy,' it called. 'You've got number 1 right. Number 2 should be 88, not 8 as you have it. Number 3 is 44 . . .'

Suzie was amazed. 'The answers sound right,' she thought.

'Number 4 is 4, the square root of 16,' it continued. 'Number 5 is 17 minus 5. Number 6 is 2002. And number 7 is completely impossible.'

'I thought it was!' Suzie was beginning to like this creature after all. It was extremely clever.

'Thank you. That's the fastest my homework's ever been done.'

The sewer creature sighed with relief. It did a kind of slippery dance, stretching and bending its brown spots as it leapt through the air. It looked so comic that Suzie exploded into laughter that echoed round the chamber.

'Then let's start all over again,' it said, out of breath, 'and I'll say how you can help. But first let me introduce myself properly. My name is Harold Foot-Webb. I'm a Sludge-Gulper, from the East End.'

A slimy wet hand was proffered.

Suzie clutched it with great difficulty, for it

15

was cold, clammy and as slippery as snail slime. But she said politely, 'I'm Suzie Stanmore. I'm eleven, and in class 1B at school. What would you like me to do?'

CHAPTER THREE

Queen Greenmould

'The situation down here has reached crisis point, because of Queen Greenmould,' Harold Foot-Webb explained.

'Queen Greenmould? Who on earth is she?'

'You mean, who *under* the earth is she? Well, listen and I'll tell you.'

Suzie sat on a relatively dry ledge, using her maths book as a cushion.

'Queen Greenmould is Queen of the Sludge-Gulpers. She lives in the sewers directly below Buckingham Palace, and copies *everything* your Queen does Up Above. She's a dreadful snob – in fact her whole court are snobs. They won't touch any food from the Royal Drains unless it has "By Appointment To Her Majesty The Queen" on it. When your Queen has a Garden Party, Queen Greenmould holds a Sewer Party.

When the Queen Up Above confers honours, Queen Greenmould does the same.'

Suzie giggled. 'She sounds great.'

'No, you're wrong,' said Harold Foot-Webb seriously. 'Her snobbery covers up something far more sinister that's going on down here. She's a dangerous operator. Let me try to explain.

'Once Queen Greenmould was an ordinary Sludge-Gulper, born in the East End, like myself. But there was something unnatural about her from the very start. She demanded to be spoiled. She gave herself airs. She thought she was special. Her first big plan was to marry Upstream. In preparation, she swallowed a bottle of blue ink every day, to make her blood appear Royal Blue. Having blue blood makes one eligible to marry into the Royal Sewerage.'

Suzie giggled again, but this only agitated the Sludge-Gulper more.

'Please attend! At last she saw her chance, and grabbed it. She cleverly got herself invited to a "do" at the Sewer Palace, and threw herself at Prince Gropius. He has excellent blue blood, of course, from the Royal Regency Sewers of Brighton. The Brighton Sewerage is ancient: it stretches back ever so far. Greenmould knew Prince Gropius was weak and lazy. All he did was swagger around looking posh, then go out to bet on the Rat Races. He was so gullible that it was easy for a cunning schemer like Green-mould to simply flatter and tickle him into a proposal of marriage.'

Suzie laughed. She couldn't help liking this Royal Family. But Harold Foot-Webb paced round and round Suzie, exasperated, treading on his own webbed toes.

'You must understand the gravity of the situation. Hear me out! Unfortunately, old King Jodhpur passed away. His son, Prince Gropius, became King. Greenmould had got exactly what she wanted. She became Queen – and she gained *power*. This was when the trouble started. The Brighton Palace, under the Royal Pavilion, wasn't good enough for her – it was living below Buckingham Palace, or nothing. So they moved. Then the London Palace wasn't grand enough. So she enlarged it. Then she began to change *us* around. Up until recently, the sewers had always been free. The Monarch acted as our figurehead. Now Queen Greenmould wants to rule over us herself. She is dividing the sewers up. Only if sewer creatures obey her every command will she award them territory where they can eat – or "Grazing Rights" as she calls them. Her operations have been so artful and sly that we didn't realize quite how dangerous she had become. Usually, all such major territorial decisions are undertaken by Parliament.'

'You have a Parliament, too?'

'Of course. It's held directly under yours. Manhole lids are dropped all over London to summon creatures to Parliament. But Greenmould is doing her utmost to undermine our Government's part in ruling. She wants total control. How is she getting it? Setting Sewer folk against Sewer folk, that's how. For example, she's sending the Slime-Grubbers against us if we don't do exactly what she says—'

'Who are the Slime-Grubbers?'

'Slime-Grubbers are green, long-tailed creatures with claws and scales and rows of sharply pointed teeth.'

'They sound nasty!'

'They used not to be, but we never know how they'll react nowadays. Their leader, Bounders Green, has become very nasty indeed . . . Oh dear, I must make things clear. Once, you see, everything ran along smoothly in the sewers, every creature doing its job. Sludge-Gulpers gulped the sludge, Slime-Grubbers chewed slime from the walls, and the Rats scavenged on anything else. We existed quite happily side by side. The sewers were kept clean and worked with efficiency. Now Queen Greenmould has stirred everything about. Groups of Slime-Grubbers are being trained to spy on Sludge-Gulpers. They smell you out, and they can swim through the strongest currents after you. And she's tempting the Rats to join her – by offering them extra territory. She doesn't act like a proper queen – more of a dictator. But we Sludge-Gulpers will never be subjected to her will.' Here Harold Foot-Webb stamped so hard that Suzie had to dodge the sludge.

'Can't King Gropius stop her? He must have some control over her. After all, he is the King.'

'Gropius? Poor King Gropius is useless. The moment Greenmould ascended the throne, she nagged him till she drove him to drink. Nowadays all he does is lounge about boozing. He's grown as soggy as a cesspit. He no longer loves the Queen, but showers all his affection on their daughter, Princess Griselda ... And there's a problem. An airlock in the pipes.' Harold Foot-Webb's face was swamped with a scowl of anger. 'That despicable Bounders Green intends to marry Princess Griselda so he can eventually inherit the throne – but I love her, and we're secretly engaged. She's very wonderful. Her beauty knows no bounds ...'

Here Harold Foot-Webb went all peculiar. His eyes rolled, the end of his nose grew damp, and he blushed so that his brown blotches joined in a medley of orange. Suzie sighed. She'd seen this sort of thing recently between Miss Penge, the music teacher, and Mr Richmond, who taught them geography.

'And you're worried you might lose her?'

'Exactly.'

Harold Foot-Webb's skin took a while returning to its normal colour, but as it did so, he grew correspondingly despondent. 'But really it's not just my personal problems I'm worried about. You see,' he croaked in a low voice, as if he might be overheard, 'I think Queen Greenmould is actually going mad. Somehow I have to convince the others that her reason is crumbling. She's indulging in crazy things – like forcing her daughter to pinch things from Up Above.'

'What kind of things?'

'Things owned by the Royal Family. A plastic paddling pool belonging to one of the grandchildren, a corgi's eating bowl, a royal toothbrush – mostly things that are blue. On discovering that Her Majesty's favourite colour is blue, Queen Greenmould insisted that hers was, too.'

'How did she find that out?'

'By listening up the drainpipes. She's even developed a posh accent by eavesdropping up the Queen's own plughole. She heard her in the bathroom practising her speech for Christmas television.'

Suzie tried desperately not to explode with

mirth, but the Sludge-Gulper now looked very serious indeed.

'You must understand, Suzie. Obsessive snobbery, combined with power, makes a lethal mixture – a mixture more dangerous than anything. For hundreds of years we've managed to keep ourselves secret from Up Above. But supposing they investigate? Just imagine . . . if we were *seen?* Humans would think us vermin, wouldn't they? We'd be *exterminated!*'

Now Suzie fully understood his alarm. She fidgeted nervously.

'You've kept yourselves incredibly secret up to now. I've never heard of sewer creatures, and there aren't any fairy stories about you . . .'

'We've not been discovered – yet. But Greenmould's getting greedier. Every new raid is an extra risk. At Christmas, for example, she got poor King Gropius to creep up and steal fairy lights from Christmas trees all over the Palace. Then she got *me* to connect them to the mains electricity supply. Now they adorn the Sewer Palace. The Queen loves them. It doesn't cross her mind for an instant that she's clocking up your Queen's electricity bill. She's even had Christmas parcels stolen from round the tree Up Above. Your Royal Family received very few presents last year – the Royal Family Below had tons. Your Queen must be wondering—'

23

'She'd be too polite to complain about presents. Anyway, she said on the television that she is quite looking forward to her retirement.'

'Ah! Now I can explain how we need your help. You see, Queen Greenmould has modelled her whole life on your Queen. As far as she's concerned, your Queen can do no wrong. So what in Hounslow she'll do once she finds out that her heroine had decided not to rule any longer – well, it's just too frightening . . . You see, what you must know is that I am Prime Minister . . .'

'Oh!' said Suzie, smoothing her skirt and sitting up straight, now that she knew how important he was.

'Being Prime Minister means that I spend most of my time at our Parliament. Now no one knows Up Above, but there's a leak in your House of Commons just below where the Conservatives sit. If I crawl along a narrow pipe, I can put my ear to a tiny hole below the benches to overhear Parliamentary debates. I've been following, step by step, Up Above's dissatisfaction with the Royal Family. Months ago I sensed what was likely to happen – a vote in which your people could choose between a Monarchy or a Republic. Now, I'm the one who brings Queen Greenmould the Parliamentary news, and I know she shouldn't be told.'

'She's bound to hear about today's Abdication before long. Everyone knows about it,' said Suzie anxiously.

'She's aware that they've had rows and there's to be a vote – but she thinks it's on "Home rule for Scotland". When she does find out, I fear she'll flip her lid. Maybe she'll do something absolutely earth-shattering, like try to get her own back on your Queen. I can imagine her shouting abuse up the plughole, for example. The Queen Up Above would shriek out . . . the bath would be dug up – and what would she find underneath? Oh, it's too terrible even to contemplate.'

Harold Foot-Webb suddenly slumped like a punctured tyre, staring, with his filmy eyes fixed on an imaginary future – an awful time, where every sewer creature had been violently flushed away.

'I'll help,' said Suzie quickly. She no longer felt like laughing. 'Tell me what I can do.'

'Thank you!' The Sludge-Gulper looked really relieved. 'It was so dangerous for me to get in touch with a Human; but I had a feeling this crisis could not be tackled only from Down Below. But Suzie, I must be able to trust you. Will you stand on Storm Alert? Will you promise to keep our identity a secret – even if things get dangerous? Swear "Foot in the Sludge".'

Suzie was about to swear, but had no chance.

'What's that?' she cried, as an infernal racket rose above the flow of sewerage from along the dark tunnel – a grunting and squealing and splashing that echoed louder as it approached.

'Quick! Hide! I mustn't be seen with a Human, or the Queen will suspect a plot. No! Don't hide in the lift either,' he called, as Suzie tore towards it. 'No one must know about that. Get behind this ledge. And don't budge an inch!'

Suzie barely made it. She crouched, shivering, as the squealing grew louder. Then she saw her exercise book, left lying on the ledge where anyone could see it. Judging by the noise, something vast was just around the corner, so she stayed hidden. Suddenly the creature appeared – it was a very small, totally white pig. Suzie almost laughed out loud. It approached with considerable speed, squealing to warn of its importance, looking straight ahead with little pink eyes. Before it disappeared Suzie noticed a soggy *Daily Telegraph* in its mouth, clutched between its short front teeth.

'That was a pig! What's a pig doing down here?'

'Oh dithering dishwater! That was the Swamp Pig. He was heading straight for the Palace and the Queen. I'd forgotten she'd put him in charge of the Gutter Press. He's got wind of what's going on and he's taking her the news right now! I wonder if I can head him off? Look, Suzie, we've no time to make any plans. Will you come with me? I've got a torch I stole from the Flushers Up Above. It'll help you see in the gloom. Wait here while I get it – I hung it on the back of your lift. If we're quick, we could take my short cut to the Palace and get there before the Pig.'

Suzie could only nod her consent, rather nervously . . . as the torch was fetched, switched on, and lit up all the sludge.

CHAPTER FOUR

The Greenbacks

T he moment Suzie shone her torch into the sewer's dismal mouth she hesitated. Her slender beam of light lit an eerie pathway that went on and on until it was swallowed in darkness. Nothing seemed still. Her torch made swarms of silver blobs, which danced in ripples over the moving water and were reflected in long stretched shapes on the curving walls. And everything was so damp. Glistening brickwork seemed to ooze like an over-filled sponge, and moisture sweated its way through mouldy growths dangling from above.

As Suzie stepped rather gingerly into the sludge, she realized what she was taking on. Going right inside the tunnel was scary. She followed as close as she could behind Harold Foot-Webb.

'Smells a bit rough at first,' the Sludge-Gulper

said cheerfully. 'Acrid, but not unpleasant. You'll soon get used to it. Besides, there's plenty of warm soapy water to help things along. It's not all stuff from the lavatories – there's effluent from baths, launderettes, the washing-up. Half a million gallons pass through the bowels of London Town every day, and all of it ends up sooner or later being processed in the Great Works at Beckton. Come along, we're going too slow.'

'But don't you all feel terribly ill living here?' Suzie asked, trying to speed up, whilst not looking too hard at the greyish scum that surged by.

'Absolutely not. Strong, robust and slimy are the Sewer Creatures. The odour contributes greatly to our general health.'

'How on earth do you know where you are? It must take ages to learn.'

'It's not that hard. Tunnels always join up – in the Centre at least. Beyond that, things are different. Some say there are thirteen thousand miles of sewers. Others say, there is no end. You can usually tell where you are Under London by the smells. Of course there are sewers of different degrees of repulsiveness. Under hospitals are to be avoided. Under Smithfields is pretty nasty, too, with all the straggly bits from the meat market. But other sewers are plain fun – like the Dye Works near Beckton. Sometimes the young

Gulpers whirl around in the different colours that get sent along. Then they go back home, startling their parents stupid by turning up all bright orange, pink or mauve.'

Suzie chuckled. It was such a different world down here that she found it hard to remember that the London she knew was overhead. Mostly they travelled deep down, but occasionally, when they came closer to the surface, rays of blue poured like misty moonlight from roadside grilles or larger ventilators, allowing the ghostly roar of traffic to be strained down. It was as if the manholes were lids into her world above. She tried to pick up sounds from Up Above. A police siren fading into the distance, a bus starting up – all funnelled down through a drain-pipe.

For a time they climbed gently, until they reached a junction where four streams met. It formed a chamber, built with high, wide ledges and metal rungs, leading to a large, square man-hole overhead.

'This is an Expansion Chamber. It takes the extra flow when it rains. Normally we could rest here before taking the main sewer running under Buckingham Palace Road straight to the Sewer Palace. Today there's no time to rest. Also I plan to approach Greenmould's Palace from the back, travelling below Belgravia, then clipping the end of the Knightsbridge sewer before turning to go underneath Buckingham Palace Gardens. We should catch up with the Pig just as he reaches the Palace. The Flushers Up Above set up all sorts of metal bars to stop Humans from getting near your Palace via the sewers, but I've rigged most so we can slip through. The Pig takes a long detour to avoid them, because he finds it difficult to crank up the bars with his teeth. We should just be able to beat him. You've done well – very well, Suzie.'

Suzie glowed with pride. She wasn't complimented often, and she grew more confident. Mostly the sewer tunnels were round, but sometimes there were raised edges at the side that you could walk along. Soon she could slide and balance through the tunnels beautifully – even wade fast through the sludge in the middle. 'Maybe it's because I'm brilliant at gym,' she thought. 'I bet Jane couldn't do this half as well!'

Suddenly a jet of hot, foaming bathwater gushed from a smaller outlet high on the side of their tunnel.

'Watch out! We're under the French Embassy! This is where we turn east.'

Suzie just managed to jump aside to avoid being engulfed. The water was filled with the best French perfume, and bobbed off downstream in tiny islands of froth. 'I bet that person doesn't know I've seen the other end of their bath,' she thought.

'Travel faster, if possible,' urged Harold Foot-Webb. 'If we're to head off the Pig.'

'I'm going as fast as I can. Tell me how the Swamp Pig got down here,' she asked, to stop him hurrying her any more. 'And why is it so white? Pigs are usually pink.'

'The Swamp Pig got flushed down. Most things found here have been flushed down. The Swamp Pig was pink once, of course, but creatures who are not used to the sewers always turn white after a while. There's so little light, you see. Other than some small sewer spiders, thin white worms and woodlice, the only natural inhabitants of the London Sewers are the Sewer Rats, ourselves and the Slime-Grubbers. Even the Alligator got flushed down.'

'Alligator? There's a real alligator down here – as well as a pig?' Suzie grew alarmed. A small pig was one thing, an alligator quite another matter.

'Yes, he was flushed down when small – probably someone's pet, but when no longer wanted, conveniently flushed away. Grown too much, perhaps. That's what usually happens. That's why these unfortunate creatures are usually so angry – because they weren't wanted any longer.'

Suzie suddenly felt rather 'flushed down' herself. Her father certainly hadn't wanted her. Why else would he have gone off to be with Miss Snaresbrook? Now it felt as if Mum had no time for her either.

'Of course the Alligator's enormous now,' Harold Foot-Webb continued. 'He's called Pompey and belongs to Queen Greenmould. He guards her palace. Don't worry, he's always chained up.'

Suzie was not reassured. 'Well, I do hope our Queen doesn't hear him at night when she's in bed.'

'No, sound doesn't travel Up Above from Down Below. You never hear the sewers, do you? Ah, here we are. This small tunnel runs right under Buckingham Palace Gardens and joins the main sewer in front of the Palace. This is where we can cut him off.'

But as they rounded the next bend . . .

'Oh, Epping and Ongar! I didn't know there'd be Greenbacks here!'

They had chanced upon a small group of long-tailed, ferocious-looking, newt-like creatures crawling about, busily grazing layers of mould from the walls. Beyond them was a series of bars forming one of the security gates around the Palace. Because they had been talking, Suzie and Harold Foot-Webb had failed to hear the noise of grinding teeth.

'Are those Slime-Grubbers?' Suzie whispered hoarsely.

'Yes!'

Suddenly a huge bunch of Suzie's hair was grabbed by Harold Foot-Webb's damp fingers, while his other hand forced her head down.

'Switch off the torch! We need to get past these Greenbacks. Pretend you're my captive. I mustn't be seen with a Human whatever happens. Not a squeak out of you until we get safely by!'

Next, a blood-curdling bellow split the air, shattering in echoes against the sewer walls. This was followed by a squeal of annoyance.

'Blistering bung-holes! That's Pompey bellowing at the Pig – he's beaten us to it! Trust those Greenbacks to cause a delay. We'll have to go to my secret hiding-place straight away. From there we can spy through a hole in the wall right into Queen Greenmould's Palace. At least we'll be able to see what's going on.'

The Prime Minister hurt Suzie badly as he dragged her along, but she dared not complain. Out of the corner of her eye, she saw some of the creatures stop grubbing the walls, to turn and grin, showing yellow gums as they curled back their snouts. A few female Slime-Grubbers guarded eggs. They whipped their tails, and glared from mean-looking eyes set far too close

34

together. Baby Grubbers clung to their mother's backs and chattered tiny teeth together for practice.

Gradually they sidled past without causing trouble, until they reached the security gate. With his free hand, Harold Foot-Webb cranked the bars upwards, pushed Suzie roughly through, and cranked them down again. They were safe.

'Now, climb this disused Tumbling Bay. It'll take us inside an abandoned Inspection Chamber. It's derelict because it was considered too much of a security risk, being so close to the Palace Up Above.'

The Tumbling Bay was just a series of concrete steps. Suzie switched her torch on again to mount them. Then, down a side tunnel, her beam picked out the huge shape of a dark monster, with thrashing tail and glistening scales. Suzie also glimpsed a clanking chain that snaked from a hook on the slimy wall, before she was ushered into the Inspection Chamber, shivering as she rubbed her bruised head.

CHAPTER FIVE

The Sewer Palace

'Come up this end, Suzie. Look, you can see everything inside the Sewer Palace!'

Harold Foot-Webb had uncovered a chink in the brickwork, and, as Suzie put her eye to the hole, she forgot her fear of Pompey. She could hardly believe the fantastic vision. There, in one great blaze of fairy lights, was the Royal Throne Room, looking like a perpetual Christmas Day.

The walls and ceiling were covered with dried-out mud which had cracked into a maze of finely-crazed lines, sparkling with rainbow colours from the lights. Plastered all over the mud, Suzie saw silver spoons, broken china, sardine tins, golden rings, silver from cigarette packets, nuts, bolts, diamond necklaces, children's toys and plastic flowers . . . all stuck or dangling from rootlets above. A great tree in Buckingham Palace Gardens must have broken into the sewer at some stage, for its roots curled and twisted to make all sorts of seats, arches and alcoves.

And there, enthroned on a special root in the middle of it all, sat Queen Greenmould, ruler of the London Sewers. To one side of her, a mud fountain played, sending a froth of cool silty foam on to her royal webbed toes, which twitched slightly as she leaned forward to receive a soggy newspaper from the snout of the little Swamp Pig.

Suzie had thought that Harold Foot-Webb was rather tubby, but so vastly overweight was Queen Greenmould that, as she patted her Pig, the mouldy green splodges, stretched tight across her toadish form, joined together in a roly-poly of shivering folds. On her fat head was wedged a crown constructed from many extraordinary things – amongst which, Suzie detected tooth-brushes, tinsel and an egg-timer. In one hand she wielded a sceptre (which looked suspiciously like a plastic lavatory-brush). Behind her, two gulping maidens fanned her vigorously while she read the headlines.

Suddenly the Queen rose up, gave a huge gulp and wildly thrashed her arms.

'*How dare she!*'

Her Majesty collapsed back on to her Throne

Root, while ladies-in-waiting rushed forward to waft spray from the fountain over her face.

'*Abdication! Retirement! How could she!*' She roared. She struggled to her feet again, flushed scarlet with indignation, while her maids supported her. The little Pig trotted quickly to hide behind the fountain.

'*She may be abdicating in favour of a republic! I most certainly am not! I am carrying on!*' At this decision, Her Majesty felt distinctly better. 'Where's King Gropius? Where's Princess Griselda? Where's Harold Foot-Webb?'

'Out, Your Majesty.'

'Then I must do all the thinking myself, as usual.' And she began to sway about the room, swishing ladies-in-waiting away with the lavatory-brush, and muttering furiously.

Suzie and Harold Foot-Webb craned forwards to hear what she was saying.

'And what will happen to her crown? Her sceptre? Her orb? Her purple vestments? Her throne? All now no longer needed. *She* may be giving them up . . .' She paused. '*But I won't! Court, attend! If Her Majesty Up Above no longer wants her Royal Regalia . . . then I, Queen Greenmould, will have them!*'

'Oh no!' Harold Foot-Webb covered his face in his hands. 'That's precisely the kind of thing

I *thought* might happen. She has gone quite, quite mad.'

'Where *is* that Prime Minister? Why is he never here when one wants him nowadays? Why didn't he inform me of this? He keeps disappearing. Go and find him. *No!* Clear the Court . . . Fetch me instead Bounders Green, leader of the Slime-Grubbers!'

There was some disturbance as the Throne Room was evacuated. Then a shiny, bright-green creature entered, swishing a long scaly tail from side to side, as he bowed before the Queen.

'Bounders Green . . .'

'Yes, Your Majesty?'

'It seems that Her Majesty Up Above is retiring. She has no further use for her orb, sceptre, crown and throne. Would it be possible for you to help me obtain them?'

'That's a highly difficult request, Majesty,' he replied in a high-pitched, sawing voice. 'Almost impossible. In fact it would involve enormous risks.'

'Then maybe you will be able to do it . . . say, with the help of a "title" – like, for example, *Sir* Bounders Green?' said the Queen, feeling her way carefully.

'What about complete control of the Grazing Rights of Mayfair and Knightsbridge, Majesty?'

Queen Greenmould scowled. But she had to grant the high price he was asking. She nodded.

'That makes it somewhat easier, Majesty. But it would have to be some really well-plumbed scheme . . . and it would take a lot of daring. But I think I *could* invent something.'

The scaly creature grimaced, bowing obsequiously as he curled back his snout to smile. Suzie saw ferocious yellow fangs, and a treacherous set of teeth.

Harold Foot-Webb groaned and backed away from the hole. 'We've got to stop him – but we need all the help we can get. I'll have to inform the others. We must hold an Emergency Meeting straight away. Come on, I'd better take you home. It's getting late.'

On the journey back, Harold Foot-Webb was far too despondent to speak, and Suzie could think of nothing but visions of the Queen's Royal Regalia disappearing down the drains. When they reached the lift, Suzie realized that she didn't know how to contact the Prime Minister again.

'There's only a week before Abdication Day. If the Emergency Meeting comes up with a plan, how can we get in touch? Will you send me a note or something, when you want me to come down to help?'

'No, too risky. You've no idea the difficulty I had pinning that note to the lift. It must be a signal . . . Yes, I have it! You know that manhole in the middle of the road, opposite the letter box near your school?'

Suzie knew it only too well. It was the very manhole where she'd first seen the Sludge-Gulper.

'Give three knocks on it every day after school. If I answer, it means you're to come at once. I know what time school finishes.'

'OK,' said Suzie. 'I'll tap on it every day.'

Suzie decided to hang her sewer torch back behind the lift – her mother might ask questions if she took it home. Then she got into the lift quickly – in case, upon departure, it was polite to shake hands.

CHAPTER SIX

Edna Pongworthy

Mr Morden, the maths teacher, peered curiously at Suzie over his glasses. It was Jane's homework that Suzie usually copied – he was well aware of that. This time was different. Not only were all her answers correct (Jane had numbers 3 and 5 wrong for a start), but this child was the only one in the whole class who had pencilled firmly 'Impossible' against question number 7. All the others had tried to make some bungling attempt at it. He was impressed. Afterwards, everyone wanted to know how Suzie had got number 7 right. She kept quiet.

When walking home from school, neither Clare nor Jane could understand why Suzie would run to the centre of the road in Sutherland Street, do an odd kind of tap-dance on the manhole cover – wait, as though listening, then carry on as if this were perfectly normal. They didn't like to say anything, but secretly they both thought she was going mad.

Then, coming home on Tuesday, it happened. After the tap-dance, Suzie spun off and ran down the road, without even saying goodbye. On her face was a look of panic. What's more, both Clare and Jane were convinced they'd heard three sharp raps coming from *underneath* the manhole cover. Still, they thought, strange things were happening everywhere, with only a few days to go before British History changed for ever.

Much of the country was still against the ending of the Monarchy. There were protest marches as well as heated debates in the House of Commons – everyone was suffering from the frenzied speed of events. The Queen had asked just one thing: that she might be allowed to retire quickly and quietly. But Parliament had declared Abdication Day a bank holiday for the whole nation. Friday was to be celebrated in a big way.

Mrs Stanmore arrived home late from her day shift, tired out from all the extra work they had been given. She looked puzzled to see Suzie dressed in her anorak and a pair of wellington boots.

'Where are you off to, Suzie? And why the boots? It's not raining.'

'I'm . . . I'm helping to find Jane's kitten,' Suzie stuttered. 'It's got lost in the basement.'

'Well, that's exactly why you couldn't keep Monument. Cats that live in high-rise blocks have nowhere to play. Yes, do go and rescue it, the poor thing. Don't forget your key. By the way, I'm making a casserole for you to eat later. Work is exhausting; we've never painted mugs so quickly. You don't mind, do you, darling? Only three nights more.'

To her surprise, Suzie didn't. She was out through the door and off down the corridor. Everybody else used the normal lift. Suzie chose the service one.

'Harold Foot-Webb, where are you?' she called anxiously from the safety of the lift. No one answered. Using the glimmering light from the grating up above, Suzie was able to unhook the torch from the back of the lift. Then she shone it down the sewer's mouth. Over the sludge came an apparition in white, floating along. Suzie shot behind the ledge and switched off the torch. 'What an idiot! Why did I call out? Now they'll suspect a plot.'

' 'Ello, Suzie, is that *you* . . . *oo* . . . *oo* . . .?' a voice echoed.

Suzie flattened herself, keeping absolutely still.

'I'm afraid the Prime Minister couldn't come . . . um . . . um. 'E sent me instead,' the voice rang out. 'Don't be scared. I'm Edna. Edna Pongworthy . . . orthy . . . orthy. I've been sent to fetch you to a secret meeting of Sludge-Gulpers.'

The voice sounded friendly enough. Suzie peered out. The apparition had reached a pool of light from the next grating along, and she could see that it was another Sludge-Gulper wearing a hat and gown encrusted with tiny pearl buttons. When it reached the ledge, it grabbed Suzie's hand in a slimy grasp, and lowering its voice, croaked:

'Edna Pongworthy, friend of the PM's. All 'ell is breaking out at the Palace. Greenmould's furious with 'Arold for not telling 'er about the abdication, so 'e's staying out of sight. The important thing is that, at this very moment, Bounders Green is to inform the Queen 'ow 'e means to pinch the Royal Regalia. Princess Griselda will listen carefully, then relay the information fast to the PM, who will rush it straight to us. But things is mighty dangerous – you must be disguised to reach the meeting safe. Wear this gown and hat I've brought, then you'll

45

be safe. It's me 'usband's, and it should fit you just nice.'

Suzie slipped it over her anorak, where it hung like a tunic.

'What a wonderful gown. It must've taken ages to sew on all these buttons. Did you think of the idea?'

'Lord, no. 'Aven't you 'eard of Pearly Kings and Queens?'

'Yes, of course,' Suzie grinned. 'We've got them Up Above. I've seen them in the Lord Mayor's Show.'

'Well, it's the same down 'ere. There, you look a treat. Now the hat.'

'Wherever did you find all these buttons?' Suzie was enjoying herself, despite the danger. She loved dressing up and wished she had a mirror.

'The Sludge-Gulpers search for 'em in the sludge. Any sewer creature finding one is well rewarded. All us East Enders know exactly where to look – under Whitechapel Road, beneath Petticoat Lane. Any place where clothing's manufactured Up Above, some're bound to come down. Good! The hat fits perfect, but your lovely fair 'air'll show . . . put it all 'idden inside. You mustn't be seen – Greenmould's got spies everywhere. Even some of the Rats loyal to us 'ave deserted, tempted by bribes from the Queen.

We don't want you to be grabbed. Everything that gets flushed down is declared "treasure trove" and gets dragged to the Palace as property of the Queen. Now, girl, we mustn't waste time nattering. Let's be off.'

Suzie kept looking over her shoulder nervously to see if they were being followed. Edna offered a hand to help her along faster, but as this slipped straight from her grasp, Suzie politely declined assistance and decided to rely on her own balance. So instead, Edna sang a song of encouragement in a high, pearly kind of voice.

> 'The Sewers don't stink
> As much as you think.
> When you've been down 'ere long,
> You'll get used to the pong.
>
> It's a matter of time
> Getting fond of the slime;
> Then soon you'll feel well . . .
> Even relish the smell.'

This time, they set out north-eastwards, travelling under Victoria Station. Almost immediately, a great side sewer from a milk-bottle-washing depot joined theirs, and the two streams swirled like coffee and cream. Then there was a hollow rumbling, which caused drips from the ceiling to sheer sideways and the brickwork to tremble. Suzie cowered.

'What's that?'

'It's only a District and Circle underground train – they run quite close to where we are. Soon we'll reach the High Interceptory Level Sewer, which'll take us due east under the Mall. We used to 'old meetings under St Paul's Cathedral, but Greenmould's got spies posted there. Where we're gathering instead is a cover-up. What's 'appening looks ordinary enough. What's really going on behind the scenes is another matter. Sshh!'

'What is it?' Suzie whispered.

'Stop!' Edna frowned and put her ear to the tunnel-side, concentrating. 'I can 'ear feet. Marching Slime-Grubbers, sure as filth. Bounders Green must've chosen the High Interceptory Level to drill 'is men. Slithering soap-suds! We'll 'ave to follow the Tyburn sewer to the River Embankment then switch to the Fleet and go round that way.'

The new route took them lower and deeper. Before long, they reached an extraordinary place. The great underground channel had broadened, lifting into a high arched roof supported by enormous Gothic columns and plinths. It was like going back a hundred years.

48

Suzie gasped as her torch picked out hundreds of yellow bricks in diagonal stripes overhead.

'Magnificent, isn't it, the Tyburn sewer? That clever man Joseph Bazalgette built it in Queen Victoria's reign – nobody's done better. 'E used all sorts of sewers – egg-shaped, barrel-shaped, arched, almost square. And 'e put the narrow ends of the brick facing out, so as they'd never wear away.'

'The bricks are so beautiful. It's like an underground cathedral! *Ooo!*' Suzie sang.

'*Ooo,*' echoed from all around.

Edna smiled and clapped. Her claps echoed, and became applause, which faded away as they strode out again.

'Before Bazalgette, London was a load of old cesspits. In 1810 there was two 'undred thousand cesspools that 'ad to be emptied by bucket. I know 'cos we learned it in 'istory. Now you see 'ow delighted we was when this lot was built so long ago specially for us. The High Level Sewer from 'Ampstead took over four million bricks, they say. No wonder they made 'im into *Sir* Joseph Bazalgette – 'e deserved it.'

'Wow!' gasped Suzie. And the echoes from the Tyburn agreed.

'We first came 'ere from the East, from the 'Ackney Marshes after they was drained. Then us Swamp Creatures, as we was known, moved into the sewers and changed our name. The Rats, who 'ave always been around the Centre, were wary of us at first. But when they saw 'ow we 'elped activate the sludge, they accepted our presence. We Sludge-Gulpers mostly stick in the East – them Greenbacks consider the West their territory.'

'Where did the Greenbacks – the Slime-Grubbers – come from?'

'Migrated in from the West. River-folk they was once. They say they developed from large green river newts. I reckon they've got a bit of crocodile in 'em!' Edna laughed.

Soon they reached the Thames Embankment and travelled along parallel to the river. Here they had to plough through many smaller tributaries which kept joining theirs, flowing down from Central London. One of these delighted Suzie by shooting down a stream of Alphabetti spaghetti, closely followed by some long wormy pasta.

'That'll be from that Italian restaurant in the Strand. There's some Indian stuff comes down further along.'

Edna decided to turn northwards before reaching the Fleet – it would be quicker. As they waded upstream against a narrow, swift current, Suzie started to tire. Her wellingtons became two sodden weights. And she thought she heard gnawing and squeaking from the smaller outlets on either side.

'Rats! I can't go on,' she whispered, for she had glanced up a side-tunnel and caught sight of the younger ones playing some kind of Rat-race along the sewer walls.

'Don't let them upset you, Suzie. They'll not 'arm you. As soon as they 'ear noise, Rats scamper off. 'Old on, girl, we're practically there.'

'Yes,' whispered Suzie in a fragile voice.

'You should get used to Rats – try to respect 'em. They're essential to the whole sewer system.'

So Suzie had to learn about Rats.

'The common Sewer Rat is quite small, but there's a lot of 'em because they will breed every twenty-eight days. They've got soft bones, so they can squeeze through the smallest outlets that lead to your 'ouses, where they find most of their food. Rats love fat most, and fat is the cause of most blocked sewers, so they do useful work under cafés, where sausage-and-chips is the order of the day. There are some very large, powerful Rats, too – the Gourmet Rats – who only eat under posh hotels and restaurants on a diet of fancy five-star food. Then, of course, there's the Company of Grey Rats ... but no one ever sees those. They are mysterious, silent creatures that live below Westminster, and are said to 'ave special powers. You don't want to get on the wrong side of them, so steer clear at all times.'

Uncomforted by her new-found knowledge, Suzie quickened her pace until the scuffling was left behind. Turning sharp west, they entered a warm, damp, medium-sized sewer under Covent Garden.

' 'Ere we are!' announced Edna, with relief. And she knocked loudly on a metal door which said above it:

SAUNA SWIMMING BATHS WASTE OUTLET. PRIVATE. NO ADMITTANCE.

CHAPTER SEVEN

The Sauna Baths

S uzie stared open-mouthed at the wonderful
scene before her. They had entered a kind of
underground swimming pool – or more of a
grotto, since phosphorescent algae, glowing
bright aquamarine, covered both ceiling and
walls. Sludge-Gulpers of every size and descrip-
tion bathed, wallowed and slid down slimy
slopes, pitching into swirling pools, sending up
sprays of mud into the billowing steam. A
broken hot-water pipe, travelling along below
the silt, had formed a kind of geyser-line which
erupted in a series of blurps, like bubbling porridge. From their turbid centres, dreadful
swamp-fogs momentarily curled, blotting everything from view. Through a clear patch, Suzie
saw infant Sludge-Gulpers blowing bubbles of
fine silt, or gurgling in the steam under the super-
vision of their nannies.

'Well, 'ere we are, Suzie, right under the Sauna Baths at Covent Garden,' cried Edna, as they were surrounded by excited, swampish creatures, dancing and grinning.

'You made it! You made it! Well done, Suzie – we've 'eard all about you.'

''Ow about introducin' us to yer friend?' said a comfortable matronly Sludge-Gulper wobbling up. 'She don't half look boiling 'ot in all them clothes, poor fing.'

'Oh, I *am* sorry,' Edna apologized. 'You can take those off now, Suzie. This is Jacusi, keeper of the Baths.'

'Hello,' said Suzie. 'The pearly gown's got dirty. I'm sorry.'

'Never you mind, girl, they'll come clean in the baths; then them buttons'll shine up somethink luvelly. It's a smashin' Cover-Up 'ere, ain't it?' Jacusi whispered. 'Behind the baths, the *real* meetin' place is 'idden down the Inspection Chamber!' she divulged, pointing through the steam. 'None would know though, would they? The PM's expected any minute now.' And she wobbled off, bearing away the gowns.

Just then, a serious-looking Sludge-Gulper came up.

'Suzie, meet my 'usband, Purley,' said Edna. 'And don't forget to thank 'im for 'is gown. 'E's never lent it to no one before.'

54

'Pleased to meet you, I'm sure,' said Purley Pongworthy, politely accepting Suzie's thanks. Now at last, Suzie didn't flinch as she gripped his hand. She had discovered how to do it the right way: you clasped hands, then squeezed hard until they naturally slipped apart.

Behind Purley Pongworthy were two very old Sludge-Gulpers, sitting side by side in what Suzie thought were immense rubber armchairs . . . until she recognized them to be two inflatable dinghies with LONDON WATER AUTHORITY printed in large letters down both sides.

'Suzie, this is Grandad and Granny Gulper – true Cockney Pearlies. Both born within the sound of Bow Bells – below grating, that is.'

''Ow do you do,' croaked Grandad, in a voice ancient as the drains. ''Ow are you keepin', luv?'

'Very well, thank you.' It was true, Suzie didn't feel too bad at all, considering.

'And I'm Mother-of-Pearl.' Granny heaved with silent laughter.

'Don't mind 'er,' chuckled Grandad. 'She's antique. Sometimes 'er mind is like mud, she can remember nuffing. Other times, the silt clears right away and she remembers right back to the Big Stink.'

'Big Stink did you say?' echoed Granny Gulper, querulously. '1858 it was. Nasty. Everything got thoroughly bunged up. You could

55

'ardly breathe for the stench. Sumthink awful it was.'

'I love your armchairs,' Suzie said politely.

'Grand, ain't they? They got nicked from the Flushers. All our best stuff comes from their Inspection Chambers.'

'Lazy sogs, most o' them Flushers. Real wets. Only bover to come down inspecting every three or four years. Then they paddle along nice an' easy in them dinghies, as if they didn't want to get their feet damp.'

Suzie liked Grandad and Granny Gulper. Their fingers were covered with rings of plastic or glittering gold. But both their pearly garments were old and tattered; several areas had no buttons at all. Suddenly, Suzie thought how she could thank Purley properly for his gown. She unzipped her anorak (which was a relief anyway in the heat), and recklessly tore off most of the buttons from the front of her school blouse.

'Here you are, two for you, Grandad, two for Granny Gulper – and a few for Edna and Purley, in case you need them later.'

'Oogh! You're a real treasure. We usually 'ave to dredge for 'em.'

Just then, two eager young Sludge-Gulpers hurried up out of breath.

''Allo, Mum, who's this then?'

'Suzie,' said Edna, 'these are my two girls, Flotsam and Jetsam. Say 'ello.'

''Ello 'Uman Lady,' they said politely. Then, seeing that Granny Gulper's mind had cleared, they settled down at her great webbed feet.

'Granny, tell us about the olden days when everything was really foul!'

'You mean 'ow 'orrid the Fleet used to be when it was just an open sewer? Wiv bits of body an' parts of old dog thrown down to be got rid of?'

'Enough, Gran!' Edna interrupted. 'There's no time now for ancient 'istory, and I've got an important mission for you two girls. You're to wait outside where the Main Overflow Outlet runs into the Sewer. As you're young, you'll not worry any Slime-Grubbers – and you must warn us if any are about. Run and tell us quick the moment the PM arrives.'

'Oh Ma . . .'

'Now go on, or you'll get posted through to Up Above,' threatened Grandpa.

'Ooogh!' they squealed, racing away.

'Young as spring water, aren't they just?' chuckled Grandpa Gulper to Granny. But Granny Gulper had sunk right into her inflatable and her large lidded eyes were closed shut like a couple of manhole covers.

'Her mind's probably silted over,' thought

Suzie, as she crept quietly away, allowing Grandad to sing Granny a restful lullaby while he stroked and patted her hand:

> 'Wiv a mirror and some glasses
> You could see to 'Ackney Marshes
> If it wasn't for the gratings in between.'

Suzie was taken to 'freshen up' under where the main steam outlet jetted in, until she was all clean and tingly. Then at the chamber's end, she saw a bouncy-looking Sludge-Gulper doing some pressure cooking in an enormous potty.

''Allo, I'm Steaming Lil,' she grinned, 'and I'm cooking a nice Southwark Stew.' Without more ado, she proceeded to poke some rubbery bits to the surface. 'Try some, dearie. Go on, 'ave a taste.'

'No thank you,' Suzie declined – although she *was* getting terribly hungry. Luckily, Flotsam and Jetsam raced to her rescue, crying:

'Suzie's got to come along with us! The Prime Minister's arrived!'

Before you could say 'sludge', various crea-tures had slipped from the baths into the secret Inspection Chamber.

'Wakey wakey Mother-of-Pearl,' croaked Grandad, nudging Grandma and urging her along. Suzie sat between Edna and Purley, who wore their freshly steam-pressed gowns. Then Suzie spotted several large, distinguished-looking Rats sitting among the Sludge-Gulpers – she was only just able to stifle a scream. They were discreetly cleaning their whiskers, waiting for the meeting to begin.

Silence settled like sediment throughout the gathering as Prime Minister Harold Foot-Webb, still panting from the effort of his journey, got on to the platform to speak.

CHAPTER EIGHT

The Secret Meeting

Harold Foot-Webb looked very grave and official as he took the central position on the platform. But on seeing Suzie, his face relaxed for a moment into a welcoming smile.

'Fellow Sludge-Gulpers and Rats, thank you for attending this secret meeting. Many of you have travelled through dangerous areas to get here. But I'm afraid that the news I bring today will horrify you all. Princess Griselda herself has informed me that her mother, Queen Greenmould, has a diabolical plan – a plan that will put every sewer creature's life in jeopardy.'

A murmur ran through the assembly. Several creatures gulped.

'Bazalgette bless us! Whatever next?' cried Jacusi.

'I bet that scoundrel Bounders Green has something to do with it,' said an important-looking Sludge-Gulper with limpid, wrinkled eyes.

'You've guessed right, Rickmansworthy. Both Bounders Green and the Swamp Pig are involved in the Queen's plot. Princess Griselda says that this is to take place *underneath* Westminster Abbey on Abdication Day.'

Now all the creatures listened intently as Prime Minister Harold Foot-Webb unfolded Queen Greenmould's abominable plot.

It transpired that she had sent her devoted Swamp Pig to rootle around in the ancient labyrinth of drainage tunnels underneath Westminster Abbey. There, his excellent sense of direction led him to the discovery of a secret bricked-up vault, part of which had crumbled away with age. The ceiling of its central chamber ended just below the Abbey floor. (He could hear a choir practice going on directly above.) Because the Pig was the only creature who could venture Up Above safely, without causing concern, he was sent, just after dawn, to spy in Westminster Abbey. He had used a flight of stone steps leading to a manhole in the cloisters. Inside the Abbey, he had seen where they had placed the ancient wooden coronation throne (used by every monarch since Edward II), that was to be used for Abdication Day. He calculated that it was slap bang over the central chamber below.

There was a gasp of astonishment then murmurs of terror from his audience, before the Prime Minister was allowed to complete his news. The Queen's plot, he said, would now be easy to carry out. The floor of that part of the Abbey was formed from large black and white marble slabs. Bounders Green and his gang had assured her Majesty that they could carefully cut through the grouting around these slabs from below. Only a small area on the surface need be left uncut, so that nothing would show. Those marble slabs would be braced below with a cross-lattice of metal drain-rods. A large fishing net, found blocking the drains under the Old Billingsgate Market, would be unfolded to hang underneath. The moment the Queen sat down on her throne to be un-crowned on Abdication Day, her extra weight would be too much . . .

'*Crash! Wallop!* Through the floor she'll tumble, throne and all – into the net, and into the vault leading directly to the sewers below.'

'*No!*' cried Suzie.

'Lawks!' croaked Granny.

'That just about turns off the tap!' shrieked Steaming Lil.

'Calm down! Calm down! Her Majesty's not to be killed. Queen Greenmould isn't interested in her now she's gone Republic. By the time Her Majesty is rescued, the sceptre, orb, crown and throne will have been carried off in the net – dragged away by a great party of Slime-Grubbers, assisted by a gang of traitor Rats.'

For several moments there was silence, while the full impact of the dreadful scheme sank in. Then:

'Treachery! Shame!' they exclaimed.

'We'll not let it sogging 'appen,' swore Edna.

'The Queen's gone completely crazy!' exploded Rickmansworthy.

'If her insane plan goes ahead,' warned Purley, 'we'll surely be discovered, then destroyed.'

'What can we do? How can we stop her?' they all called out.

'There's only one way we can prevent her,' Harold Foot-Webb replied. 'Queen Green-mould's not stupid. She knew she had to keep her scheme a secret until she was certain of a way to capture her booty. Now that a way has been found, even the Queen knows that a majority of creatures must approve her plan. It has to be made law first, and voted through Parliament. As I am Prime Minister, I will no doubt be forced to set this up. So, what we must do is outvote her.'

'Yes! Yes!' they chorused. 'We will outvote her.'

Now the meeting broke up into small groups discussing ways of getting in the votes. But

Harold Foot-Webb banged his chair loudly on the floor.

'Pay attention, everyone. There's more. Prepare yourselves for another impending disaster . . . Before the Queen wears the Royal Regalia herself, she plans to use it first for a different occasion. The Queen intends a Royal Wedding to take place on Abdication Day Up Above. One that will expand the Monarchy Under London, and make it more powerful. By marrying off her daughter, she will strengthen her own position as Queen. But her choice of bridegroom is outrageous. She intends Princess Griselda to marry Bounders Green. She will announce their engagement tomorrow. But this wedding must be prevented . . . for I have to tell you all now that I am secretly engaged to her myself.'

'You never!' chuckled Steaming Lil.

The Prime Minister blushed so furiously that he overheated and had to stand gulping to cool himself down. At last he raised his hand to ward off other stray comments and continued.

'This is why Princess Griselda is on our side, and why she will report her mother's every move, spying without arousing suspicions, courageously putting her own safety at risk – because she loves me, and cannot abide the thought of marrying that scaly Bounders Green. Her mother is forcing her into a marriage without love.'

Next to Suzie, Edna seethed with rage. Her anger reflected in her pearls, turning them pink.

'Once upon a time Greenmould 'ad to activate the sludge just like the rest of us, didn't she, Mother-of-Pearl?'

Granny Gulper rose quivering to her feet.

'It's my fault really she's the way she is,' she croaked. 'I indulged 'er every whim. You see, she could wheedle 'er way round my little webbed finger. And as we all know, when the 'eart melts, the mind turns to mud. There was such tantrums if she didn't get 'er way. She always 'ad to 'ave loads more buttons on 'er gown. If only I'd've known what it would lead to.' Here Mother-of-Pearl broke down with a fit of the vapours.

'Get 'er away, quick! She's goin' all wimble and wembley!' cried Steaming Lil. And poor Granny Gulper was helped from the room, sniffing Grandad's sulphur smelling-salts.

Now the meeting was threatening to get out of control. Everyone tried to talk at once. But a bossy-looking Sludge-Gulper had jumped on to the platform.

'Oh no, not 'er,' whispered Edna Pongworthy. 'Not Water Loo . . .'

'Well, I know how we can stop all this. I think

we should get rid of our complete Royal Family. I'm for a republic Down Below. That King sinks his alcohol like a sump, the Queen's as fat as an overflow outlet, and Griselda's a spoilt sprat going the way of her mother. They're a load of snobs, as bad as one another. Just let me get my hands on that Princess Griselda – the *great sulphur-bellied toad*!'

'How *dare* you speak of my fiancée in that manner!' The Prime Minister had turned a nasty colour.

'Sit down, Water Loo, we don't care two buttons for what you've got to say,' yelled Edna. 'All of us is very traditional down 'ere. We've always 'ad a King and Queen. You're just as green as a water-butt, Water Loo, 'cos Princess Griselda didn't want you at Court as one of her ladies-in-waiting. You're really a Royalist like the rest of us. We agree some changes need to be made – but to go Republic . . . None of us wants a republic, do we?'

'No! No!' they yelled.

Water Loo looked uncomfortable and shuffled her feet. But then she became defiant. 'Conservative stick-in-the-muds, the lot of you,' she retorted. 'Especially Edna, who's a complete blockage. I'll persuade every creature in the sewer to vote for a Republic. We'll have a great new, powerful, super-sewer – just you see.'

There was an uneasy silence as her audience was appalled. Then:

'Send 'er packing!' screamed Steaming Lil. 'She's flowed right over.'

'Hear, hear,' agreed the assembly.

'I'll go of my own accord, thank you,' scoffed Water Loo, realizing she had been overruled – then added spitefully, 'As for Harold Foot-Webb, you're a *big drip!*'

'Out of the meeting!' ordered the Prime Minister. 'We've had just about all we can stand!'

'You'll regret this! Just wait and see!' Water Loo was about to sweep from the room in a whirlwind of foul gas, when Edna gathered her robes about her and leapt neatly on to the platform.

'Don't let her leave! She may do something daft – like go and tell the Queen about our secret meeting.'

'Oh no she won't! I have her!' shouted Frogmorton, a large blotchy-green Sludge-Gulper, who had been squeezed into the front row, but now had Water Loo floored. 'Fetch a rope and tie her up. We'll have to watch her rather carefully until the Abdication is over.'

Once the traitor was safely bound and gagged, Harold Foot-Webb said, 'Let's get on with the meeting now. I can't stay long. I must get back, in case the Queen finds out we're plotting against her.'

An old, sinewy Rat stood up, smoothing the whiskers round his mouth.

'I'd like to speak on behalf of us Rats,' he growled.

'Yes, Chigwell, what have you to say?'

'Things are getting really bad for Rats. We like to think of ourselves as intelligent creatures, going about our own business, attending to our needs. Once we lived side by side with Sludge-Gulpers and Slime-Grubbers; but the Queen's new Grazing Rights have changed all that. And there's a danger. There was a time when the Flushers and Maintenance Men from Up Above didn't have to do anything but go to the boozer every day. *We* did it all for them. Now the Flushers are wondering why some sewers have clean and shiny walls, while others are filthy but have beautifully activated sludge.'

'That's right,' agreed his friend, Shadwell. 'Gradually, over the past few years, more and more Rats have been clawed out of the sewers under Soho and Chinatown. Slime-Grubbers are taking them over. We're being crowded towards the Fleet and Tyburn.'

'What it all seeps down to,' said his wife, Angel Rat, 'is this: Soho and Chinatown have got blocked solid with fat from the restaurants.

Brave Flushers have tried pickaxes to budge it, but it's gone too hard; they've had to give up. The Flushers now think the system's gone rotten. What are they doing about it? Putting in those shiny metal liners. Only Slime-Grubbers can get a grip on them. Soon, with the entire system renewed and all Sir Joseph Bazalgette's work needlessly altered, that'll be the end of us Rats – unless we move to an entirely different sewer system miles from London – and we all know what *that* would mean.'

'Territorial wars,' squealed all the Rats, gnashing their teeth.

There was a grim silence at this terrible prospect.

'Right then,' said Frogmorton, summing up. 'We all now realize that Queen Greenmould is right round the bend with this plunge and grab idea of hers. She's risking our whole world in this bid for the Crown Jewels. If those Humans catch even a glimpse of "peculiar creatures" dragging the Royal Regalia away, we'll all be flushed out. We've got to stop her. There's to be no stealing the crown and throne, no wedding with Bounders Green, and no more territorial changes. Does everyone agree?'

'Yes! Yes!' they chorused.

'Carried unanimously,' the Prime Minister pronounced. 'So we have to devise a strategy.

Greenmould will do everything in her power to see her plot gets voted through. We must come up with a scheme to prevent it. Today is Tuesday, Abdication Day is on Friday. We've little time – so think, everybody, *think*.'

'Short of becoming builders and bricking every entrance to the Abbey *before* they get there,' said Rickmansworthy, 'there's nothing watertight I can think of.'

'I've just thought of something we could do,' said a timid voice. But Suzie – for it was Suzie who spoke – felt far too frightened to go on to the platform. She'd never been able to talk in front of an audience. That's why she couldn't put her name down for the school play, although she longed to.

'Go on luv, let's 'ear you,' encouraged Steaming Lil.

'Be brave, Suzie,' said Edna, pushing her up. 'You may ventilate your views in public like everybody else.'

So Suzie got to her feet. Shakily she mounted the platform. 'It was . . . it was the talk of builders just now that gave me an idea. My uncle Ongar is a builder. He uses props to hold up ceilings and things while he's strengthening them. They're called Acro-props. If we could borrow one from him, we could put it under the throne to prop it up *after* they've done their

70

cutting and gone away. Acro-props are terribly strong. I don't think the throne would collapse – even if Her Majesty sat on it.'

'What a brilliant child,' said Edna. 'No wonder she 'ad so many buttons on her shirt. She deserved the lot of 'em.'

'An incredible idea – but it might just work.' The Prime Minister suddenly looked himself again. 'Can you describe this prop, Suzie?'

'Well, an Acro-prop is a strong tube that you extend up or down with ratchets. It has a square plate on one end to rest it on the ground and a square plate on the other to prop up whatever you need to prop up.'

'Sounds just the ticket,' said Rickmansworthy. 'Could you get one?'

'Yes. My uncle's doing up a shop in a road on the way to school. There are several supporting the ceiling – I've seen them through the window. I could post one down that large manhole near to school.'

'Splendid, splendid,' said Frogmorton. 'Let's hope that with one of those, the throne will be secure.'

'Then I'll post it down tomorrow night after school, if you like. That'll give two clear days before Abdication Day. But I'll have to ask Clare to help – it would take two people to lift.'

'Who is this Clare? Is she trustworthy?' asked Purley.

'Yes,' said the Prime Minister. 'I can vouch for her. I've observed her.'

'I'll swear her to secrecy,' said Suzie, eagerly. 'Foot in the Sludge! I could come and show you how to work the prop after school on Thursday, while my mother's at work – that's if you or Edna promise to meet me.'

'Of course we will, luv,' said Edna. "Ow can we ever thank you?'

'By letting me go home. It's getting late and I must be back before my mother returns.'

'Couldn't she go by tube rather than sewer?' suggested Angel Rat. 'She could use that disused platform at Covent Garden, right overhead. I know a door from here that goes up there, then through on to the real platform. No one ever uses it, but it's always unlocked.'

'I haven't got any money for the tube.'

'Money? Cash? Got plenty of that stuff,' said Purley. 'Gets flushed down via the gutters every day, and we've no use for it at all. We've got ancient money, too. We've florins, ten p's, three-penny bits, two-pound coins, fifty p's, half-crowns, groats, one-pound coins . . .'

'Pound coins will be fine, thank you.'

CHAPTER NINE

The Acro-prop

Suzie rushed back to their block just in time to see her mother disappear into the lift. What could she do? She was meant to be in – homework done, supper eaten. She ran to the other end of the corridor and jumped into the service lift, thinking up the wildest excuses – none of them any good. Then she saw her mother at the end of the landing talking to Mrs Osterley, their neighbour. She was outside Mrs Osterley's doorway with her back to Suzie.

'Hello, Mrs Stanmore. You're working awfully late this evening. My dear, you *do* look tired. How's the mug painting going?'

Suzie saw her chance. Taking off her boots so they wouldn't squelch, she crept past, unlocked their door and slipped inside.

She then moved faster than the speed of light. She went into the kitchen, switched on the microwave; into the bathroom, turned the taps on full; back to the kitchen, grabbed a fork and food; back to the bathroom with supper, locked the door tight.

'Hello, Suzie, is that you? I'm back.'

'Yes, Mum, I'm just having a bath.'

'It's rather late for a bath, isn't it? I was about to have one myself.' She sounded tired and cross.

'My telly programme finished late. I won't be long.'

Suzie ate supper in the bath, ravenously, and afterwards smuggled the carefully rinsed plate back to the kitchen inside her towel. She put the anorak into a carrier bag and stuffed it under her bed.

'So that's why no one sat next to me in the tube: it smells revolting!'

But her mother had gone in to have her bath before Suzie could retrieve the rest of her things.

'Suzie! All the buttons are missing from your shirt. They look as if they've been ripped off. Suzie, where have you been? Your clothes smell as if they've been buried! And the bath is disgusting!'

'The kitten,' stammered Suzie, weakly. 'It was stuck up a very narrow pipe in the basement. Mummy, we had to get her out . . .'

Mrs Stanmore sighed as she fetched a fresh set of school clothes. She felt responsible, working late every night, not being around to care for her daughter or encourage her efforts at school. She knew Suzie missed Monument a lot. And life without a father for her must be very similar to how she felt herself, as if a massive hole existed in their family . . .

Then Mrs Stanmore discovered that Suzie had not done her homework.

'You told me yourself, Suzie, the composition had to be in by tomorrow. You said they were being marked Wednesday morning, so the best could be read in class during the afternoon. Do it right away.'

Suzie had worried about this composition for the last three days. She couldn't think what to write. The title was so soppy: 'The London I love'. She had tried in vain to write about the old house, the garden, Monument, but—

'Of course! Now I *can* do the composition. I know all there is to know about "The London I love".'

Filled with inspiration, she began to write furiously: 'There are more than thirteen thousand miles of sewers under London . . .'

A free morning had been declared at school on Wednesday so that everyone could paint new banners. These would have VALE REGINA on them – which her school said meant, 'Farewell, O Queen'.

Suzie, who had slept like a log, was strangely exhilarated. She had been pleased with her helpful suggestion of the Acro-prop at the meeting, then proud of her essay, which she had really enjoyed writing. Now she felt part of the Abdication activities, and threw herself into the preparations. First they made a huge banner out of sheeting to drape across the school entrance. Next, loads of bunting to hang from the school windows across to those over the road.

They intended to give the Queen a jolly good send-off.

In the afternoon the compositions were judged. Suzie's was top, and she won a gold star.

'It's certainly an original essay . . . if somewhat unsavoury,' said Miss Stockwell. 'However, I've checked the facts and they seem to be correct. Heaven knows where you got the information.'

Suzie had to stand and read it in front of the whole class. Normally she would have been terrified – but she'd had a little practice.

'Basil Jet built the main sewers 160 years ago, but some are even older, like the Tyburn and the Fleet, because they are really the original rivers flowing into the Thames. The smell is acrid but not unpleasant. It's not all stuff from the lavatories . . .'

'Great composition,' said Clare.

'Brilliant,' said the others.

'Well, I thought it was really horrid and disgusting,' said Jane.

But Suzie didn't care what Jane thought. She enjoyed being popular – it felt great.

'Clare, would you help me with something really important after school today? It's top secret. No one must know.'

'What is it?' Clare was proud to be Suzie's best friend.

'It's of National Importance. You must just trust me. I need help to carry an Acro-prop. It's too heavy for me on my own.'

'Sure,' said Clare – although she had no idea what an Acro-prop was.

They discussed arrangements for a while, sitting on their desks. And when they had planned their secret mission, Suzie made Clare swear, 'Foot in the Sludge', to absolute secrecy about stealing it. If her plan worked and the Queen was saved, Suzie knew she would become part of the History of Great Britain. But no one must ever know what she had done – she didn't dare tell Clare anything about the sewer creatures.

After school, Suzie and Clare went up the side street to the empty shop. Peering through the window they could see three Acro-props holding up the ceiling. Suzie concentrated for a while.

'I think we'll take the middle one. The ceiling will probably stay up without it.'

'It would be terribly embarrassing if it all collapsed,' Clare worried.

'I expect it'll hold OK. Anyway, we have the greater need.' Under her breath she added 'Extracted "by appointment to Her Majesty The Queen".'

Round the back of the house there was a narrow alleyway. Suzie decided it would take a little gymnastic skill to get over the wall. A pile of planks and sand had been left by the builders for the following day. They lifted the top plank and leaned this against the wall. Then, while Clare held it steady, Suzie ran up it on to the top of the wall and jumped easily down. She unbolted the gate and let Clare in. Now they had to get into the shop, which they thought would be much more difficult – until they found that the whole of the back part was being rebuilt and they could walk straight in. Suzie went up to the middle Acro-prop, released the pin from the ratchet, and carefully wound the prop down. They waited for several minutes to see if the ceiling would collapse – but nothing happened.

The Acro-prop was heavy, but they hauled it out, one on each end, and manoeuvred it down the road. Clare didn't quite understand what this game was all about – but it was very exciting, stealing Acro-props.

They put the prop behind a low wall and went to see if the road was clear. The manhole itself was fairly close, but there were far too many people around.

'This is hopeless,' said Suzie. 'We'll never be able to post it down without someone noticing. What can we do?'

The friends sat on the wall and thought hard.

'The Queen's Retirement Speech!' Clare shouted suddenly.

'What?'

'The Queen's giving her Retirement Speech at seven tonight. It's on radio and television simultaneously. Everyone'll be watching or listening.'

'You're a genius! Of course! Can you get away? I can. Mum will be out painting mugs.'

'Don't worry, my parents will be glued to the screen. I'll sneak out the moment it begins.'

And they were right. The road was empty. They carried the Acro-prop to the middle of the road with some effort, lifted the manhole cover, and posted it down.

*

Down in the sewers, an unhappy ceremony had also taken place on Wednesday evening, when Queen Greenmould forced Princess Griselda's engagement to Bounders Green. Poor Grisely was in a frightful state. Her fiancé – who at the same time had been given a knighthood and now insisted on being addressed as Sir Bounders Green – was round at the Palace at all hours. The Queen demanded that they 'get to know one another', but the Princess kept tripping over the foul green creature's tail, which he swished about. For his engagement present, the Queen had lavished further Grazing Territory. He had control of every sewer from Kensington Palace Gardens to Parsons Green. His friends, Kenzal, Harry Neasden and Dalston Green were given situations in Park Lane and Under Piccadilly, in exchange for which they were to help the Queen – by cutting through the marble slabs under the throne in Westminster Abbey.

In a dark side tunnel, late at night, a party of Sludge-Gulpers found the heavy steel Acro-prop where it had been posted through the manhole Up Above. They gave it a shallow grave in the sludge, in case it needed to be dug up in a hurry. They had to watch out: Slime-Grubbers were drilling their soldiers up and down the tunnels, and more and more Rats were being encouraged to join up for the Queen.

CHAPTER TEN

Sir Bounders Green

It was Thursday afternoon. Abdication Day was tomorrow. London looked prettier than Suzie had ever seen it before. Flags looped from one side of the street to the other, and people chatted about politics to neighbours they had never spoken to previously. There was an excitement, an air of expectancy – as well as an atmosphere of sadness and change – that made most Londoners incapable of work. Even school ended early. Suzie ran most of the way home because she was to go down into the sewers to help the Sludge-Gulpers with the Acroprop.

When she got back, the flat was empty, her mother out at work. Suzie no longer had that 'I'm-all-on-my-own' feeling. She was about to help save the Queen – it was the most exciting night of her life. Quickly, she rummaged for her oldest jeans and sweater. Her wellingtons she found cleaned and tidied away in the cupboard. She fished under the bed for her anorak in the carrier bag. It smelt awful. 'But I'll soon be filthy again,' she thought, as she eased it over her clothes. Finally, she slipped the 'Do Not Disturb' notice on her bedroom door, in case she was a little late.

Suzie made for the service lift which she knew would be rigged for her to go down. When it landed Under London, the Prime Minister was already there pacing anxiously. With him, Frogmorton and Rickmansworthy wriggled their feet with impatience.

'Suzie, at last! We thought you'd never come!' said Frogmorton, rushing towards her.

As they went through the usual hand-shaking, Suzie noticed a large new plastic ring on Harold Foot-Webb's finger, but was given no time to comment. There was bad news.

'Water Loo has just escaped,' said Frogmorton. 'She refused to eat, but puffed herself up whenever anyone went by. This afternoon she got thin enough to wriggle out of her ropes. No one can find her – but I expect she's headed for the Queen or Sir Bounders Green to spill the beans.'

'This makes everything more urgent and dangerous,' warned Harold Foot-Webb. 'Listen

82

to the plan carefully, Suzie. After you posted the prop down, we covered it safely with sludge. Since then, Frogmorton has located an unused sewer closer to Westminster, where we can hide it until it's needed. The Slime-Grubbers are going to cut under the Abbey floor late tonight once all the rehearsals are over. Griselda will inform us when they get back to the Palace. Then we'll be able to unearth the Acro fast, and take it to prop up the throne. However, first you must show us how it works. Will you come with us?'

Suzie was excited to be walking towards school under the ground, below territory she knew. How strange it felt – rather like knowing the 'behind the scenes' of it all . . . or rather, the 'under the scenes'.

Their route would take them north, then west to the Victoria Street sewer, leading straight to Westminster. Some distasteful fumes of diesel and car exhaust told her they must already be underneath Buckingham Palace Road – and its usual traffic jam. Then they were met by a tide of foam that crept like a slick over the surface. Steam rose from it so they were pushing through quite a thick fog. The torch was worse than useless in the swirling glare. At the same time

Suzie inhaled another smell which she could not quite identify, until:

'Of course, we must be under the launderette! And that other smell is dry-cleaning fluid.'

'Quite a cocktail of smells together,' remarked Rickmansworthy. 'It often happens that way; they are like markers for us Down Below.'

As they progressed, the Prime Minister spoke bitterly of the engagement of his fiancée to Sir Bounders Green, and of Kenzal, Harry Neasden and Dalston Green's new territorial rights.

'They're forming themselves into gangs, under orders from the Queen,' said Rickmansworthy. 'Every soldier who joins the ranks is rewarded with a special flexible pass-card to show their loyalty to Her Majesty.'

'She's successfully tempted some of our largest Rats over . . . Tottenham Court Rat, Oval, and Wapping Rat – even Squeaker Brent has deserted,' added Frogmorton, angrily.

'If Queen Greenmould forms an army,' warned Harold Foot-Webb, 'we'll be forced to defend ourselves – and that can only mean *civil war*!'

Thinking of this made them so dejected that Suzie was quite relieved when they reached the Acro-prop, and got involved in extracting it from the mud. Then, spacing themselves equally along its length, they began to haul, working up a kind of rhythm. Suzie felt a sewer-rhyme forming in her head, a hauling song to keep their spirits up.

'How many people who walk down the street,
Know what is happening under their feet?'

Before long, they encountered their first hazard – an enormous weir. Dark waters poured noisily over it, to be sucked into a Storm Channel many feet below. And there was a Tumbling Bay in full working order, over which a cascade rushed down, sending up a sea of spray. Suzie liked seeing a staircase turned into a waterfall. It would be nice to have one like that at home, she mused. But Frogmorton wasn't so pleased.

'Sogging cess-pits! I'd forgotten that weir,' he cursed.

'No effing and blinding in front of a lady, Frogmorton,' reprimanded Rickmansworthy, gruffly. 'See that railing running along the top? We'll have to steady the prop with one hand and grab the rail with the other.'

Carefully they spaced out to balance the weight, then waded over in little steps, taking care not to fall.

Many tributary sewers now entered from the sides to join the weir. Frogmorton pointed to a relatively clean-looking tunnel with shiny walls and an even flow.

'That way's towards Westminster,' he yelled above the racket.

It was while travelling along this sewer that they began to hear shrill noises, faint at first, then louder over the flow of water.

'Slime-Grubbers, marching!' warned Rickmansworthy. 'Hide the Acro.'

'Post it up that narrow tributary, quick!' shouted Harold Foot-Webb. 'You, Frogmorton, Rickmansworthy, cover it with sludge. Guard it with your lives! Suzie and I will run to the next outfall.'

Raucous singing now accompanied the scampering. This burst into sharp echoes as ranks of marching eyes rounded the bend.

'Without the Throne the Queen will tumble.
The Monarchy will surely crumble.
The sceptre, crown and orb will fall,
And Queen Greenmould shall get them all.
Hurrah! Hurrah! Hurraaay!'

Suzie dashed towards the next outfall. The entrance was slightly higher than the main one, discharging its effluent in a kind of torrent. She jumped up into it, but there was a squelching as one of her wellingtons got stuck in the mud and

86

was left behind. She pressed against the sewer wall, hardly daring to breathe, her heart pounding loudly. Harold Foot-Webb leapt quickly in front of the boot to hide it.

'They'll not dare harm *me*,' he whispered. 'Keep dead quiet! I'll try to distract them.'

The rank of yellow eyes got closer. It was a group of Slime-Grubbers, shouting, 'Who goes there? Show your flexible cards!'

Harold Foot-Webb remained silent as Sir Bounders Green stepped forward. 'Oh, it's you, PM,' he said in a familiar way, tucking a newly acquired cane under his arm. 'Of all the people in the great cesspool of London I have to bump into you. Going to the Queen, ya?'

'Yes, as it happens, I *am* going to see the Queen. And I shall be reporting your insolence to her,' replied the Prime Minister.

'Actually, I'm recruiting – under *her* orders, as it happens.'

Sure enough, another horde of Slime-Grubbers scampered down the tunnel from the opposite direction seeking to 'join up' for the Queen. In doing so, they trapped Harold Foot-Webb rather awkwardly in the middle.

'Let me pass!' the Prime Minister ordered, trying to appear calm. There was a pause while both creatures glared at one another. Harold Foot-Webb felt beads of sweat form on his brow and prickle in channels down the slime on his face. He must not let his fear show. He was aware that his loyalty to the Queen was questionable, and that his position as Prime Minister was more than shaky. The only course of action he could take was to assert his superiority over Sir Bounders Green. Quickly, he leaned forward and flicked some imaginary sludge off the Slime-Grubber's shoulder; then, looking him over, proceeded to adjust his cane, as if inspecting a guard. Then he stepped back, nodding approval.

Sir Bounders Green was taken aback by this. He faltered, embarrassed.

'Troops, divide!' he stuttered. 'Let him through.'

The Prime Minister breathed deeply in relief. Sensibly he had relied on instinct. He had correctly guessed that this Slime-Grubber had not *yet* gained enough power or authority to oppose his higher rank – but it had been a delicate moment.

Then, as the new recruits were given their passes by Kenzal, one of the Grubbers pitched headlong over a wellington boot. At the same time, a large, brown, bossy-looking creature was pressing rudely forward, trying to get to Sir Bounders Green.

'Wait!' she screeched, as she caught sight of the boot. Eagerly she pulled it up and stared at it. 'I recognize that boot. Oh yes, I do! A *green* wellington boot.' With a triumphant chuckle, she felt around the mouth of the higher outlet, and extracted Suzie with one fierce tug.

'Thought so! Yours, I presume?' said Water Loo, offering the wellington.

'By Bazalgette! What have we here?' Sir Bounders Green stormed down the ranks once more, swishing his tail from side to side. 'This is most alarming! What is a Human doing down here – and in the company of our Prime Minister?' Sir Bounders Green was beside himself with glee. Being in the company of a Human was a crime so terrible that it had never been committed by any sewer creature before. Surely it would be punishable by death?

'D'you know, I'm getting to like the look of this very much! It's just too perfect for words – I couldn't have planned it better myself!' And the Slime-Grubber clutched Suzie tightly between his scaly arms.

'She's a spy from Up Above,' taunted Kenzal, scraping Suzie's mud-spattered hair with his claws. 'And the PM's in league with her.'

The Prime Minister leapt over to land protectively beside Suzie. Sir Bounders Green was now poking her with his cane.

'Going to see the Queen, were we? Very likely!' he jeered sarcastically. 'Be gracious, dear lady, to accept a flexible pass – to show your loyalty to Her Majesty, ya?'

Suzie had to accept the card from the bowing creature, but trembled so hard that she dropped it immediately in the mud. Then Sir Bounders Green turned to his rival, smirking horribly.

'Perhaps *you'll* need one, too . . . to show *your* loyalty!' Handing him a used-up telephone card, he shouted, 'Seize them! Bring them along!'

'Wait!' called Water Loo, excitedly. 'I've just escaped from the Sludge-Gulpers' clutches. I raced to inform you that the whole lot of them are traitors, plotting against the Queen. We can kill them straight away and get rid of the filthy muck!'

She hurled herself towards the Prime Minister. But Sir Bounders Green plunged his cane between them.

'Not so fast, Water Loo. Reduce your current. No one's to lay a finger on them, do you hear? I've thought of a far better scheme. You, Neasden, Dalston, stay on either side of them. About turn. Now we are *all* going to see the Queen.'

After the Recruiting Gang had left, Rickmansworthy and Frogmorton crept out of hiding and stared in despair at the retreating forms. Now what should they do? They could not manage the prop between them.

Rickmansworthy picked up the card that Suzie

had dropped. It must have fallen through a roadside grating. It said 'Miss Arabella Finchley' on it and carried the logo of the Westminster Bank. Carefully they slotted this into a crack in the roof to mark the spot where the Acro lay. Then, leaving the prop well covered with mud, they made their way back fast to get help from the Sauna Baths.

CHAPTER ELEVEN

Pompey

Pompey was waiting to be fed. He was starving. He strained on his chain and gave some short impatient grunts and several loud bellows, while saliva from his immense jaws spattered to the ground. When he was first flushed down, he had had a tiny bellow and needed only a few Rats to eat, which the Queen secretly arranged. Those who knew of this were sworn to silence. As Pompey grew, so did his devotion to the Queen. She used him as a weapon to terrify whoever she liked.

Now that Pompey was fully grown, he bellowed for more food, so the Queen was feeding him older Rats who had retired. One or two were spirited away from their Ratary Club every night, by spiking their drinks with rat poison stolen from the Maintenance Depot Up Above. Fellow Rats thought their friends had died of drink. Pompey preferred older Rats – they were bony and crunchy. But if the Queen's clever strategy was ever discovered, there'd be a dreadful Rat Revolt. Therefore revealing this Court Secret was punishable by death.

Pompey's hungry bellows terrified the prisoners as they were frogmarched by Sir Bounders Green and his gang towards the Sewer Palace.

'I'd forgotten about the Alligator.' Suzie's voice felt strangled at the back of her throat. She had sobbed throughout the journey, growing more and more afraid of what would become of her. 'I couldn't help the boot sticking, Harold Foot-Webb – wellingtons are like that.'

'I understand about the boot, and you're not to blame,' he whispered. 'But we're in a drastic situation. That leaking u-bend, Water Loo, will no doubt have a mudbath telling Her Majesty about our secret meeting – unless we can somehow discredit her first. But it *will* be impossible to think of an excuse for being in the company of a Human – though Bazalgette knows, I'm trying. I'll be accused of treason, and Queen Greenmould will probably treat you as a spy. Really, there's very little hope for us both.'

When they reached the Palace entrance they were marshalled to the chamber that Harold Foot-Webb had used as his secret hiding-place, and thrown roughly inside.

'Into the Inspection Chamber with you – until the Queen's inclined to inspect you herself,' laughed Sir Bounders Green, slamming the door.

It was useless to think of escape, they could hear guards marching up and down outside. Suzie slumped on to the ground, exhausted, and tried to stop her mind from thinking. But Harold Foot-Webb leapt eagerly to the further end of the chamber.

'Come on! At least we'll be able to see what's going on.'

Numbly Suzie obeyed. There was nothing else to do.

The Prime Minister uncovered the chink so that they could peer through.

Some ladies-in-waiting were chatting with the Queen. Next to them, lying fast asleep in a quagmire by the fountain, was the Swamp Pig, looking worn out from all his deliveries. Then, as the ladies-in-waiting dispersed, they revealed behind them Princess Griselda, sitting on a lesser Root, her large webbed feet curled around its base to keep her on.

'Look! Over there, Suzie! That's my Swamp-Maiden,' breathed Harold Foot-Webb. 'Isn't she splendid? Lovely as a lagoon! Eyes dark as night-soil! Now you can understand why I fell in love.'

Suzie gasped – a small cry escaped her lips.

'Sshh! We mustn't be heard.'

94

Princess Griselda was *ghastly* – the ugliest thing Suzie had ever set eyes on. She was even more gigantic than her mother. Splodges of a vivid sulphur yellow tumbled one over another in rich profusion, snugly settling in a series of spare tyres which spanned her lower circumference. Her dark spotted eyes bulged like her arms and legs.

'She's . . . she's absolutely *uglificent* . . . I mean, *magnificent*,' said Suzie, quickly. Then, 'Oh!' she yelped.

'What is it? Sshh!'

'Look! Look at that Rat! He's monstrous!'

A Rat of enormous size – bigger than a cat – sat contentedly at Griselda's feet, his ropy tail knotted firmly round one of her legs. White whiskers twitched on his face. Occasionally he bared some yellowing teeth.

'That's Igor, the Princess's pet Rat. Yes, he *is* rather large, I suppose. He's a Black Rat, and he belongs to the Old English Ratocracy. There aren't many of them left. Once he was leader of all the Rats. He used to be brave, fierce and terrifying – but he's been tamed and softened by the Queen feeding him left-over shepherd's pie.'

Suzie was imagining what her mother would say if she found Suzie calmly watching telly with a great pet Rat, his tail wound round her leg, when there was a bustling and marching, as Sir

Bounders Green and his gang, and a smug-looking Water Loo, entered the Throne Room with their news. Suzie suddenly paid attention.

The interview didn't take long. They couldn't hear what was being said as both Sir Bounders Green and Water Loo pressed forward eagerly to speak. But they witnessed the Queen pull back in shock, then frown.

'One will see them straight away. Fetch the prisoners in! You are discharged!' she ordered loudly, waving them off with her sceptre.

'Quick, down again!' whispered Harold Foot-Webb, closing the chink. And they were huddled in a heap by the door when it was roughly opened.

'The Queen will see you now, spy. You too, PM.'

Sir Bounders Green ushered them into the Throne Room, and hurled them at Queen Green-mould's feet. He was beside himself with glee.

Suzie looked up at the Queen's harsh face. It was plug-ugly. Most of the folds on her cheeks had plunged to form enormous jowls which seemed to munch every time she spoke. Her breath was as foul as the drains.

'So, you're a spy from Up Above are you, Human girl? And you, Prime Minister, were found in league with her by Sir Bounders Green. You're both sentenced to death.' The Queen's huge face loomed towards Suzie. 'This is an out-rageous action. My husband and I do not approve of such crimes.'

Suzie opened her mouth to cry out, but her throat was rasping and dry. She began to shake uncontrollably. Harold Foot-Webb hung his head and said nothing. He looked wretchedly drained and abject.

'Well done, Sir Bounders Green. You certainly deserve to win Princess Griselda for your reward. Now, Prime Minister, Water Loo informs one that you have been plotting against the Throne. This is sheer treachery. For that you'll receive the death sentence again. Water Loo, step forward. What would you like as a reward?'

The exultant Sludge-Gulper curtsied ungainly in front of the throne. 'To be a member of your Court, Majesty. It's all I've ever dreamed of.'

'Kneel in the mud, then.' The Queen hit her on both shoulders with her sceptre. 'Arise Lady Loo.'

'Muck-raker! Guttersnipe!' Harold Foot-Webb swore. 'You *did* want a position at Court all the time. I knew you were really a Royalist. Pah!' he spat.

But the new Lady-in-Waiting stood up, tri-umphant, and stepped back, smoothing her thighs with satisfaction.

From her root, Princess Griselda realized the danger. She dredged her mind deeply for a way to save them. But Lady Loo was bending to whisper in the Queen's ear. Her Majesty grinned, pulling her jowls into hammocks on either cheek.

'One thinks that to be a most interesting death sentence. Lady Loo suggests you both be fed to Pompey. He hasn't eaten yet. They say he's frightfully hungry. Take them both along!'

'No!' cried Princess Griselda, surging from her throne towards her secret fiancé, dragging the Rat behind. The Swamp Pig opened his eyes and gave a great snort.

'I think it an admirable idea,' sniggered Sir Bounders Green, puckering his snout in ridges right back to his eyes. He grabbed at one of Grisely's fat-rolls as she tumbled by, but she lurched deftly from his grasp, hauled Harold Foot-Webb to his feet, and, murmuring instructions in his ear, hastily brushed him down.

'Firstly, Mother, you cannot believe that your own Prime Minister would be stupid enough to reveal himself to a Human. Secondly, Harold could not possibly have been plotting. He's been with me all the time, working out this wonderful surprise for you.'

Harold Foot-Webb swayed unsteadily, but once the sludge had been wiped from his body, he regained his ministerial composure. He stood next to the Princess and said indignantly:

'Your Majesty, Lady Loo's accusations are quite preposterous! Would you believe her above your own daughter? I am not a traitor!'

'Sorry, Prime Minister Foot-Webb, one no longer trusts you. You have been behaving *exactly* like a traitor.' The Queen urged her daughter away from him impatiently with her brush, but the Prime Minister persisted.

'Your Majesty, yes, this girl *did* come from Up Above, but she isn't a spy – she was flushed down from Pimlico. Griselda and I found her yesterday while we were out taking the sewer-air together. Naturally we spent some time taming her and cleaning her up. Today, I was in the process of bringing her here to you, as Treasure Trove.'

The Queen narrowed her eyes and looked from her Prime Minister to the Princess, con-sidering this new information. She loved *presents*.

'Sir Bounders Green, were the Prime Minister and Human coming in this direction, to see me?'

'Well yes, they were, but . . .' The Slime-Grub-ber stuttered, looking suddenly rather awkward and confused, while Lady Loo's mouth fell open.

'Griselda and I thought you would be intrigued, you see,' the Prime Minister pressed home his point. 'She's a One-Off, I assure you. You'll never get another Human being flushed down.'

'Mmm. Stand before me, child. Yes, one sees exactly what you mean, Prime Minister. She does look a little unloved – but has distinct possibilities of being trained.'

'She has such a pale face, Majesty. Long pale hair, very blue eyes – everything you most admire,' Harold Foot-Webb pointed out.

Suzie gasped. She felt she was going to faint. What on earth was the Prime Minister up to? Was he betraying her to save his own skin?

The Queen prodded Suzie with the sceptre and made her turn around.

'She's certainly lovely and white. Naturally my husband, King Gropius, will have to approve her when he gets back. She'll need cleaning up, but she *could* become my Hand-Maiden . . .'

Suzie was horrified. Her so-called friend was selling her off like an object from an auction sale. She shot a wild, pleading look at the PM and the Princess, but they were both smiling broadly at her.

'I'm not white! I'm . . . pinkish,' she retorted, suddenly furious.

'So, she can speak as well, can she? Insolent child – do not contradict the Queen. You are most pale. Well done, Prime Minister. One

100

realizes that one was a little hasty to think you disloyal. We would like her.'

The Prime Minister bowed. 'I'm so glad you're pleased, Your Majesty. You'll soon be able to tame her to your needs. By the way, I hear you want me to set up Parliament tonight so that you can pass a special vote. This I am most eager to do . . . But first I need to ask you for two favours.'

Deftly, the Prime Minister grabbed hold of Lady Loo and forced her down hard into the mud. 'Lady Loo must be flung into the cooler at once. It was quite transparent that she lied in order to be made a lady-in-waiting. She's far too much of a danger to be left rumour-mongering in your Court.'

'Granted!' announced the Queen, and she waved a spluttering and resisting Lady Loo off to the cooler with her sceptre.

'My second request is rather more personal. Before I finally hand your Hand-Maiden over, may I also be officially engaged to Princess Griselda?'

Her Majesty stared, first at him – then at Suzie, weighing her new possession up. Suzie scowled horribly, and the Queen burst suddenly into peals of laughter, slapping her thighs, shaking her rolls of spots one over the other.

'Oh capital, capital, very droll. Ha ha! I will

certainly accept her. And you and Sir Bounders Green can *both* be officially engaged to the Princess – but he who serves one best will get her.'

'Then here is your engagement ring, Grisely dear.' Harold Foot-Webb beamed. His face passed through a rainbow of colours like bath-oil on water as he drew the large plastic ring from his finger and plunged it quickly onto Grisely's little finger – the only one it would fit.

'Oogh! Scrumptious!' the Princess gleamed.

Queen Greenmould peered jealously at her daughter's ring and frowned as she fingered her own, given by King Gropius – but only made of diamonds and gold. Griselda's new ring was blue, her favourite colour, and had a pink plastic heart with LUV embossed in the middle.

Radiant as a radiator, Grisely clasped her toad-like hand to her own heart and, pushing her spotted cheeks into a puffy grin, allowed her eyes to glow like pools of yellow ditchwater.

'Thank you, Squidgy,' she gulped. 'Thank you, dearest PM.'

'Well, this audience is at an end!' roared the Queen. 'Everyone is discharged! Prime Minister, you may go off and prepare for Parliament. Pig, you may accompany him to see he behaves – ha ha. You, Princess Griselda, may sew those newly-pinched plastic roses on to the train of your wedding dress, which my Hand-Maiden will be taught to carry. As for you, Sir Bounders Green, you and your Slime-Grubbing friends have to prepare for that little 'job' one needs you to do once Parliament is over. If it is done successfully, your chances for Griselda will rate very high indeed . . .'

Sir Bounders Green was livid. He'd been made a fool of. The Prime Minister had managed to twist everything around, and he, stupidly, hadn't given the Princess a ring. Neasden, Dalston and Kenzal Green looked nervously at one another, They hadn't expected this turn of events. Sulkily, Sir Bounders Green marched his retinue from the room.

Suzie sat slumped on the ground, dumbfounded. She stared at the mud fountain slurping away. Harold Foot-Webb must have planned this all along – using her as bait to achieve his engagement to Princess Griselda, whilst humiliating Sir Bounders Green. That ring he'd fiddled with all day on his finger, surely it had been there, ready to give to his fiancée? He had betrayed her horribly. She would have to stay down here for ever and ever, turning whiter and whiter like the little Swamp Pig. What would it feel like, being a Hand-Maiden in the sewers?

Suzie looked up and found herself alone with the Queen. She burst into floods of tears.

CHAPTER TWELVE

The One-Off

'Stop leaking and pull yourself together, Hand-Maiden,' ordered the Queen. 'One is rather pleased with you. First of all, you will be allowed to make my bed.'

Suzie sat where she was and looked around imploringly, but nobody came to her rescue. It was useless to resist – what could she do? The Queen was having no nonsense, she pulled at Suzie's hair.

'Come along, One-Off!'

They went down a corridor which had a ONE WAY ONLY traffic sign, stolen from Up Above. The Queen's bedchamber consisted of a tangle of arching roots that served as a bed. The bed-stead was covered in a canopy of plastic flowers, tastefully arranged. Over it was pinned another traffic sign, CUL-DE-SAC. The blue plastic carrier bags which made up the patchwork duvet, she learned, had been stitched together by Grisely's own hand. The stitches were miles apart and rather wild in their efforts to join the carrier bags together in some kind of crazy motif. Every wall of the bedroom was plastered with one-pound, five-pound, ten-pound, twenty-pound – even fifty-pound – notes, stuck on with slime. Each had the side depicting the Queen's head showing, and was placed artfully so that her portrait made an attractive pattern – sideways, upside-down, the right way up.

'Next, you will spit and polish the drips off the Royal Portraits,' ordered Her Majesty, as they walked down a tree-rooted corridor, along which some mildewy pictures hung. Suzie was impressed despite herself. The portraits were remarkably good, and looked as if they had been painted with a mixture of bath-oil and green algae. But their tour of duties was interrupted momentarily by an almighty bellow which shattered dried mud off the ceiling. This was followed by a dreadful crunching.

'That's Pompey having tea. Oh ha ha ha, that might have been you!'

Suzie felt faint, but said nothing, because they had reached a door with GRISELY'S ROOM – BEWARE OF THE RAT, nailed to the lintel.

Her walls were papered with used tube tickets, going back at least twenty years. Over her bed a notice hung saying, DANGER! CHILDREN CROSSING. Another promised, 6D A GO. Her bed-curtains consisted of pink toilet paper hanging in festoons. Suzie was astonished to see that it must be from the Queen's private chamber as it said on it, BY APPOINTMENT TO HER MAJESTY THE QUEEN. NOW PLEASE WASH YOUR HANDS.

When the Queen proudly switched on the bed-room lights, Suzie was startled by two Belisha beacons, placed on either side of the bed, which immediately began to flash on and off. Princess Griselda's duvet was made in the pattern of a zebra crossing, stitched with black dustbin liners alternating with white pedal-bin liners, from one side of the bed to the other. Her other piece of bedroom furniture was a station weighing machine going up to 80 cwt. Over the back of this, Suzie glimpsed a pearly wedding gown hanging ready for the following day. The train was frightfully long. A pile of plastic roses was waiting ready to sew on. The Princess must still have been sending her new fiancé off to prepare for Parliament.

'You will have to make the Princess's bed as well, but Igor will help. He's good at holding the covers with his teeth.'

'Yes, Your Majesty,' Suzie trembled. 'And will I have to feed the Rat?'

'No, Grisely feeds Igor. No one else may touch

him. After that, you'll polish the plastic, clean the—'

Suddenly they were interrupted by a strangled gurgling coming from Up Above.

'Quick!' shrieked the Queen. 'It's time for my bath. Your Queen is finishing hers. Hurry, child, hurry!'

Into the Shower Room they dashed, through a curtain of hundreds of paper-clips and hair-pins joined together. Hurtling down from the plughole Up Above, came the Royal bathwater.

'Don't just stand there! Take off one's crown! Scrub one's back!' She thrust her sceptre into Suzie's hands as they were deluged. 'You need to be quick, you know. Oh good, it's a bubble bath – she always has one of those before going out. I catch her singing as she pulls up the plug. I know all her favourite tunes.' The Queen grabbed the sceptre back from Suzie and hummed, 'God Save Our Gracious Me' as she brushed between her toes.

'It's a good thing the water's going out and our Queen can't hear,' thought Suzie. 'It would give her a nightmare.' Aloud she said, 'Maybe she's attending a Retirement Party. They say our Queen is actually looking forward to her retire-ment. She's going to live quietly in Sandringham, away from it all.'

Queen Greenmould reddened with rage and

appeared to swell. Bubbles from the Royal foam burst into sprays of lavender around her head.

'What utter detritus! Your Queen may be retiring,' she roared in a sudden frightening fit, 'but *we* are carrying on! I have far more *go* in me, don't you think? Answer me, child!'

'Yes, Your Majesty,' Suzie replied weakly, as the supply of water thinned to a dribble, then fizzled to a scum. The bath Up Above was empty. Queen Greenmould was very wet, shiny and clean – so was Suzie.

The Queen called for one of her ladies-in-waiting.

'Foulness! Foulness! A towel at once! Oh there you are, Foulness. You'd better make that two.'

When Suzie saw that the towels Lady Foulness brought had BY APPOINTMENT TO HER MAJESTY THE QUEEN on them (so did the toothbrushes, egg-timer, plastic train, corgi identity tag – everything on the Queen's crown), she realized that all Greenmould's possessions had been stolen from Up Above.

'She must be really crazy to have taken so many risks – or made other people take them for her,' she thought. 'Oh dear! I must escape – there has to be a way. I'll have to play along for the time being, while watching for a chance.'

'Now, Foulness. Inform the Court to prepare for joining Griselda on her honeymoon to the

Royal Brighton Sewers – after she marries one of her fiancés tomorrow evening . . . ha ha!'

'You can't go on someone's honeymoon with them,' Suzie protested.

'Hand-Maiden, one does not contradict!'

'All the real snobs visit the Brighton Sewers every summer,' insisted Lady Foulness, to prevent further argument. 'It's the Summer Recess. We go beneath the Brighton Pavilion for a change of odour, or creep out under the Pier at night. And when there are storms at sea, there's up to eighty million gallons of excess flow to bathe in.'

'And lots of fish 'n' chips come hurtling down.'

'Flotillas of French fries.'

'Soggy brown batter and Brighton rock.'

'Blue plastic buckets and blue plastic spades.'

'Picnics out at the Portobello Treatment Station.'

'Bathing in the Albion Overflow under the most wonderful brickwork.'

Flapping the sopping wet towels, Lady Foulness and Queen Greenmould danced around together singing:

> 'There's little bits of fish and chips
> With plenty of salt by the sea.'

They were interrupted by a loud fanfare, played superbly on an old portion of mains water-pipe.

'Gushing geysers! That's His Majesty returned,' cried Lady Foulness, clutching the towels and making a hurried retreat.

CHAPTER THIRTEEN

King Gropius

There was a frantic rush as the Court assembled. Queen Greenmould and Princess Griselda managed to reach their Throne-Roots with only seconds to spare, before His Majesty lurched in, dragging two large plastic buckets behind him.

'Bung-ho, everybody. Bung-ho!'

'Gropius, you're drunk!' admonished the Queen.

'Nonsense, Mouldy dear. Only had a small swim in the brewery overflow under Tower Bridge, nothing more serious.' He burped loudly, attempting to sit on his throne – a wooden barrel cut into a seat, upholstered with leather purses. 'Hello Sludge-Wumpf,' he waved to the Princess.

'And you've brought back bottled stuff. Where did you get that?'

'Crawled up the drain of a wine cellar under

Holborn Viaduct. They'll never miss 'em. Got thousands more, burp.' He grabbed a bottle from one of the buckets, wrenched the cork off with his lips and gulped, draining the bottle to the dregs. He flung the empty with expertise into the outlet from the mud fountain, watching blearily as it bobbed off down the sewer out of sight. 'Ah, that's better.'

Suzie stared at His Majesty in dismay. He looked and acted like the kind of fat, old-fashioned uncle who, deciding not to grow up, lives in a fantasy world of his own. He was a darker brown than the others, but his skin, already mottled and sagging, was so thin in places that his purple blood showed through. A collection of watches, rusted to a standstill at different times of the day, hung on a cable round his neck like ancient medals. They rested on an enormous beer stomach. Obviously he drank his way through every day, oblivious of anything. He'd be useless to prevent a disaster.

'Who's this?' He stared at Suzie, through bulging, bloodshot eyes.

'One's new Hand-Maiden, flushed down from Pimlico, Up Above. She's a One-Off. If you approve, we'll keep her. Don't just stand there, girl, curtsey to His Majesty.'

'Eh-heh. Ahem. Yes, she'll do. She's rather good.' King Gropius picked a cigar from one of the buckets, rolled off the mud between his fingers, chewed away the end, and lit it with his methane gas lighter. 'Ghastly foul cheroot, eh what?' He winked at Suzie. 'Steal 'em from the Cigar Museum under St James's. Filled with ancient pleasure. All handmade, all five years old.'

Suzie couldn't help feeling quite sorry for the old buffoon. He must suffer horribly, married to the Queen.

'Stop prattling on, Gropey. In fact, everyone in Court is to stand to attention,' the Queen ordered. 'I've two important announcements to make. Fetch Prime Minister Foot-Webb in here immediately. Fanfare, please!' The mains pipe blasted out as Harold Foot-Webb was escorted in, fully washed and oiled. He nodded to the Queen, meaning all was prepared.

'Listen most carefully! Parliament is to be held tonight. One has the most vital plan to put to the vote. It is an earth-shattering scheme that will enrich every one of you. It is essential that you all attend – I need you to vote in one's favour. In fact it is an order.'

Her court shuffled uncomfortably and there were murmurs. Surely the Queen couldn't *force* them to vote for her plan? But none dared oppose her command. To do so would throw their very lives in jeopardy.

'Second fanfare, please. Our daughter, Princess Griselda, is now officially engaged to Sir Bounders Green of Mayfair *and* Prime Minister Harold Foot-Webb. She will marry one of them on Abdication Day, tomorrow, in her pearly gown.'

The Court broke into polite applause at this rather confusing information. The Queen swivelled round to see the King's reaction, but he had turned to his daughter and was chatting to her.

'Betrothed to two people at once, Sludge-Wumpf? A well-plumbed situation – most watertight! Two's always better than one, eh?' And he grabbed a second bottle. 'Here's to a dozen more tiny swamplets. Then we can enlarge the Family Tree. Hand-Maiden, have you seen our Coat of Arms and Tree?' King Gropius waved a bottle proudly towards a heavy banner, hanging from a high root. 'You will observe that our Family Tree goes right back into the Brighton Sewerage and gets very involved. Our Coat of Arms is more simple; its heraldry shows three drainpipes noir round a bend sinister, engrailled with a rampant emblazoned Sludge-Gulper regardant a cross lozengy Ratois improper and a Slime-Grubber relaxant and slipped vert.'

'Lovely!' said Suzie. *Ugh!* she thought.

Suddenly there was a tremendous rumbling from the Queen's interior.

'It must be almost supper time.' She bent to pat her Pig. 'And our favourite meal is the same as the Queen's Above, isn't it?' she crooned. 'Let's go and see if any shepherd's pie has fallen through.'

'That pig needs far more fattening, if you ask me,' King Gropius commented, as he scrutinized the rumps of the retreating pig and Queen. 'Needs to be fat as possible before Abdication Day if it's to be roast pork, eh, what?' The King collapsed into chuckles.

'I do believe they mean to *eat* him for the wedding breakfast,' thought Suzie in sorrow. 'How *could* they eat their own pet?'

'Daddy,' pleaded Griselda. 'May I go without supper? I need to slim to get into my pearly wedding-gown, for marrying Squidgy tomorrow.'

'Nonsense!' exclaimed the King, slapping her plump thighs. 'You're nice the way you are. Tell me, Swampling, what would you like for your wedding present? Something from Up Above? How about a fat Royal corgi?'

'Don't you dare! That would be far too dangerous to dredge. Besides, Her Majesty Above might hear him barking up the drain-pipe.'

'Supper's ready!' yelled the Queen from the dining room.

Everyone rushed there in time to see a vile porridge of small lumps drowned in a rich brown gravy shoot from some shaky plumbing and slurp into a plastic paddling pool in the middle of the dining-room table.

'Sit, everybody,' commanded the Queen. 'You be next to me, Hand-Maiden.' She gestured towards the table, which was formed by a long sinuous root, supported by countless yellow road-beacons. 'As you will observe, one's dining room is cunningly placed directly below the Royal kitchens. In most places, the food comes down swimming in liquid, but in Her Majesty's private apartments, they've one of those disposal units where everything travels all nicely whirled into a delicious mousse. There's plenty for everyone. Luckily they can't all have gone out tonight Up Above.'

Suzie watched in agony as everyone sat and greedily ladled shepherd's pie into plastic corgi bowls before gobbling it down. 'So this is what I'll be eating.'

She tried to concentrate on something else to take her mind off the foul food: the 'decoration' on the sideboard, which consisted of a carefully arranged bone over a bed of marbles; the film posters with wilting corners which served as wallpaper; and above the guardsman's bearskin busby and the hand grenade on the mantelpiece, the two crossed oars labelled SERPENTINE. NOS 26 AND 7. DO NOT REMOVE. Then she saw Queen Greenmould take out a bottle of blue ink and pour some discreetly into her food. 'That's to keep her blood Royal Blue,' she thought. 'Oh dear, all of them are so fat already, even the Rat. And when King Gropius belches, the stink of alcohol from his enormous beer stomach is horrid.' Suzie attempted to catch the Prime Minister's eye, but in vain.

'Eat up, Hand-Maiden! We are all waiting,' ordered the Queen.

It was no use, she'd have to eat it. She stared into her corgi bowl and despaired. Pieces, not quite ground up, floated to the top: bits of old *Daily Telegraph*, a chewed-up bootlace. And she was so hungry. Feeling sick, she dug her spoon into the mixture, while her other hand felt in her anorak pocket for a handkerchief. Then her hand closed over a long cardboard tube. 'The Smarties!' she breathed. She'd forgotten about the bribe for Jane. Surreptitiously she drew them out. Here was something she could eat. But the Queen had noticed.

'What have you there, One-Off?'

'Smarties, Your Majesty,' she answered helplessly.

117

The Queen had seen Smarties packets flushed down, but never a full one. And among the pretty round beans were lots that were blue.

'One would like those at once, Hand-Maiden, for a pudding.'

'Yes,' Suzie whispered faintly, surrendering her supper.

'Mmm! Delicious! Here . . .' Keeping the blue ones for herself, the Queen passed the rest down the table until they ran out.

As Suzie watched the last real food she thought she'd *ever* eat disappearing for ever, she could bear it no longer. She had never felt so angry in her life. She jumped up, flung her supper to the floor, and screamed:

'You evil, stinking, scummy, selfish, monstrous, raving-loony Queen!'

Then she started running as fast as she could.

There was a gasp as Suzie's abominable insults caused the spots on the Queen's enormous bulk to rush together, then disperse into a scarlet rash.

'This is *outrageous!* Stop her! *Seize her*!' she thundered, pointing at Suzie's disappearing form with her quivering fork.

Chattering their teeth and making shrill warlike calls, a horde of Slime-Grubbers scampered after her. Before she had even reached the Family Tree, Suzie was floored, as her anorak was snatched by green scaly claws. Then she was dragged back to be dumped below the overbearing bulk of the Queen, who, still using her fork, pronounced her sentence.

'*Feed her to the Alligator at once! Let him tear her apart!*'

Above the confusion, Suzie heard Harold Foot-Webb's voice shouting:

'Your Majesty, Pompey has only just eaten, remember? Far better to shut her in the Inspection Chamber and guard her. There she can tremble all night, then Pompey can have her for breakfast.'

'A useful suggestion, Prime Minister . . . And one has just thought of an interesting *use* for the One-Off later on . . .'

The Queen herself escorted the prisoner to the cooler, watching with obvious pleasure as Suzie was hauled along by her hair, then hurled into the Inspection Chamber.

There she saw her new lady-in-waiting, Lady Loo, bound up and still sobbing. Queen Greenmould ordered her release, then taking her aside, made a secret pact with her.

'Go to the Rotten Boroughs, south of the river, Lady Loo. Winkle out every vagrant Rat you can find. Give each a voting paper. Get them to vote for me in Parliament. You have an hour in which to succeed. Sweeten the Rats with offers of new "Garbage Rights". These will tempt them . . . and I have only just this moment made them up. It is essential, you see, for my vote to succeed. For doing this you will be pardoned.'

CHAPTER FOURTEEN

Parliament under Parliament

L ong after all the maintenance men had left
the sewers and gone home; exactly when
Big Ben struck nine, there was a fearful racket.
Manhole covers were raised, then dropped, all
over London, summoning sewer creatures to
attend Parliament under Parliament. So loud was
the noise this made, that Parliament was always
called while Big Ben chimed. Its bells concealed
the row.

Queen Greenmould had reached Parliament
first, and was already seated in the most promi-
nent position on the Front Bench, so that she
could dominate the proceedings. This was to be
the most thrilling moment of her career, and a
great turning point in Sewer history. While she
was still alone, she looked around with satisfaction at the ancient Parliament with its medieval
pillars and pieces of crumbling masonry from

which the occasional gargoyle grimaced. She thought of the Sewer's long history stretching back in time, then of its glorious future which she, Queen Greenmould, was about to create. She cast her mind back to her lowly position as Sludge-Gulper Greenmould, born under the East End of London.

'How I have climbed and climbed,' she gloated, rubbing her slimy hands together. Next time Parliament was held, she would be in complete control. Wearing full Royal Regalia, pinched from Her Majesty Up Above, she would be able to dominate the lesser sewer creatures from her position of absolute power. But she knew that before this could happen, she would have to persuade a majority of sewer creatures to vote for her proposal – which she had decided to call 'Operation Royal Regalia'.

For countless years, the Sewer Parliament had been modelled on Parliament Up Above. One side of the House was taken by the party in power, the other by the Opposition. To make a new law, first a proposal had to be voted through the first assembly, the House of Commons, then ratified – or confirmed – in the second, the House of Lords. But Greenmould had made *quite sure* she would win. Lady Loo's Rats collected from the Rotten Boroughs would swell the number to vote her proposal through the Commons, and, as only those with titles were allowed to vote in the House of Lords, well . . . Queen Greenmould had cleverly *just* created a new list of titled creatures – in return for their sworn help to carry out Operation Regalia itself . . . in a few hours' time.

As Sewer Creatures from every region under London began to press into Parliament, filling every shelf, squeezing on to every ledge, the Queen was beside herself with glee. But although there were a great many Slime-Grubbers and Rats assembling on her side of the House, Lady Loo and her Rats had not yet appeared. And Her Majesty's smile turned to a frown when she looked across at the huge mass of Sludge-Gulpers and Rats which had now waded in to take up their seats for the Opposition.

'Order! Order! Order!' shouted the Squeaker Rat, and the atmosphere could have been cut with a road-drill when, after Prime Minister Harold Foot-Webb rose from his seat next to hers and opened the proceedings, Queen Greenmould was motioned to give her speech.

Like a great rubber inflatable she stood up. Then, freezing the House into silence with a withering, laser-like stare, she waited until it was absolutely still.

Carefully and enticingly, she described her plot. The priceless Royal Regalia and throne, no longer needed for the Republic Up Above, would be stolen to enrich the Sewer Palace Below. This new treasure, she proclaimed, would first be used to enhance the Princess's Royal Wedding, with all the pomp and splendour it deserved, making it into a National Triumph for the Monarchy. It was to be the beginning of a Great New Sewer Age. Finally, Queen Greenmould promised to extend Grazing Rights to under the very outskirts of London, offering rich pickings to all deserving subjects . . . once they had given her their vote.

'I have called my proposal "Operation Royal Regalia". One commends this bill to the House.'

'Hear, hear' came cries of greedy gloating from her side.

'Shame! Shame!' came those from the Opposition.

'My Honourable Lady, surely you will be *seen*?' shouted Rickmansworthy, Leader of the Opposition.

'Indeed we won't,' the Queen insisted. 'Trust me. I've taken care of all that. Sir Bounders Green and his peers will construct a special contraption on which the throne and Regalia will be pulled away by a crack team of Rats. All they'll see Up Above will be a few tails – and they are quite used to those. And I have, recently, been given a One-Off Human girl, which I intend to leave caught in a net by the hole. Naturally, they'll blame her.'

'Order! Order!' screeched the Squeaker Rat, trying to quieten the row which the Queen's speech had provoked. 'You're as bad as the Honourable Members Up Above.'

Sir Bounders Green himself rose to second the Motion. A heated debate followed, during which Harold Foot-Webb saw more and more creatures being swayed by greed and thoughts of glory. He knew he must hold back no longer. He could pretend no more to be a loyal supporter of the Queen. He rose to his feet and, changing from his Safe Seat next to Her Majesty, strode over to the other side of the House. Amid the outburst that followed, Queen Greenmould spluttered with rage and indignation. What was *her* Prime Minister doing joining the Opposition! But there was nothing she could do to prevent him – as he began to deliver an impassioned speech against her. Heroically he stood with one arm held aloft.

The Queen's desperate plan, he warned, would bring disaster. Obviously Up Above would investigate further. Every creature would get flushed away. As for her proposed Grazing Rights underneath the outer Suburbs – these sounded attractive, but what about the creatures who already lived there? What would *they* have to live on? It would bring nothing but *civil war*.

'Honourable Members,' he bellowed, 'are you really greedy enough to trade Her Majesty's offers of more territory for the safety of the whole Sewer? Have you all taken leave of your senses? Is this *really* what you want to see for the future of your Sewer?'

The Prime Minister delivered his speech with such force and outrage, that at its conclusion his webbed hand shot forward involuntarily and grabbed the ceremonial mace (which was a rubber plunger for unblocking sinks), and shook it right in the Queen's face. A gasp of horror hissed through the House, and when the plunger was returned to its rightful position, its suction pad stuck on to the damp surface, causing its wooden handle to thwack and quiver dizzily to and fro.

But it worked. The House was swayed by the powerful oration. One after another the creatures raised their hands to vote. As they were being counted, the Queen saw imminent defeat. Lady Loo and her Rats had failed to appear. Maybe her lady-in-waiting had not forgiven her for being flung in the cooler earlier on. Her eyes closed into slits, narrow as pavements cracks. She shuffled uneasily on her seat, and a smell so awful emerged from her, that everyone had to bring down their arms to hold to their noses.

Then she gave a yelp. *There* was Lady Loo, whipping a disreputable-looking horde of Rats into the House. From behind the back benches they scurried, a poor and wretched, ungroomed group.

'Disgraceful!' squeaked Angel Rat. And her call was taken up by Chigwell, Shadwell and all their loyal Rats in a symphony of squeals, then strengthened by the Sludge-Gulpers in a cacophony of croaks. But these Rats had a perfect right to vote. They delivered their soggy papers and raised their paws to be counted. There were enough. The Opposition had 103 and Her Majesty 104. The Royal Bill was passed.

Harold Foot-Webb seethed with anger and disappointment as the Operation Royal Regalia Bill left the Commons at great haste, despatched to the House of Lords to be ratified and become law. All around him, the House of Commons was evacuated with a great deal of movement and bustle, and the proceedings resumed in a chamber positioned directly under the House of Lords. He knew that Prime Ministers were not allowed to vote there. But this would give him valuable time to think. So he sat unmoving, his brain racing through various plans and possibilities.

The Queen was jubilant. She sat herself down with a loud squelch on the soggy wool-sack and called:

'Where are one's newly titled subjects? Come forward to vote, my privileged Slime-Grubbers – Lord Kenzal Green, the Honourable Harry Neasden and the Duke of Dalston. Come forward to vote, my newly titled Rats – Viscount Wapping, Sir Tottenham Court Rat, the Honourable Oval Rat, and Baroness Squeaker-Brent.'

'Turncoat Rats! Load of Slime-Grubber Wets!' jeered a great crowd of creatures who had just taken up their seats in the House of Lords. Now it was the Queen's turn to look alarmed, for every Pearly creature had arrived *en masse* from the Sauna Baths, able to vote because of their Titles. Even Granny and Grandad Gulper had managed to come. They quickly posted their votes into the House of Lords Chamber Pot.

The Queen made a mental count. She had not reckoned on her father and mother being able to make the journey. If the Bill was thrown out at this stage, she would be back to square one. *She must not be outvoted.* Sir Bounders Green and Lady Loo had just placed their votes inside. The Chamber Pot was overturned, the slips of paper were counted.

When it became clear that the vote had resulted in a draw, pandemonium broke loose.

The Squeaker Rat flailed her paws in the air to no effect, and the Queen was beside herself with fury. She inflated her cheeks and looked around. Then her face relaxed like a dose of salts. She heard a snuffling close to her own webbed feet and found a solution right there – a brilliant one. She would bequeath a title here and now.

'You, Swamp Pig!' she called. 'Step forward. For services rendered to Queen and Sewer in the Gutter Press, I create you "Sir Pig Without Porkfolio".'

She gave him a sharp whack on the shoulders, deftly smeared his snout with some of her Royal Blue ink and pressed it down on a spare voting paper. Without more ado, she folded this up and, before any objections could be made, flung it on to her pile of votes.

'If you care to count these now – you'll find that we have won.'

It took a while for the Squeaker Rat to calm the uproar, but at last, amid great suspense, there was a re-count.

The Queen had won. Operation Royal Regalia could officially go ahead the following morning.

'See, I was quite right,' crowed Lady Loo. 'Prime Minister Foot-Webb *was* a traitor all the time.'

'Yes, Lady Loo,' the Queen admitted. 'And now no one shall get in the way of my plans.

Get Prime Minister Foot-Webb in here at once. Silence the House, Squeaker Rat!' the Queen shrieked.

You could not hear a drain-rod drop as Harold Foot-Webb was ushered in, frowning deeply and with bloodshot eyes. The Queen pointed an accusing finger at him and announced emphatically:

'Because you dared to oppose me, Prime Minister, you are *sacked*! Your services in the House are no longer required. Your position shall be conferred on Sir Bounders Green.'

Harold Foot-Webb's worst fears had been realized. He felt he'd lost the future safety of every creature Down Below, as well as all hope of marrying Griselda. He had also lost his power. There was only one way out.

During the cheering as Sir Bounders Green went to the Queen to receive his new post, Harold Foot-Webb went over to whisper urgently to Rickmansworthy.

'Have courage, my friend. We must fight back with everything we have. You must go back to the Sauna Baths and start to form an army. I am going to enlist the support of the only creatures I know who have enough power to help.'

Before a startled Rickmansworthy could quiz him further, he had quietly drained away.

Once the new Prime Minister had received his

position from the Queen, he looked over to see that his rival was no longer there.

'Sludge-Gulper Harold Foot-Webb is missing!' he cried out. 'And he is now a traitor to the Queen, ya? He's bound to cause trouble – even raise an army. We should pull the plug on him right away.'

'Exactly, Prime Minister!' the Queen retorted. 'Form a force right away to track him down. Put out a big reward for his capture. Five hundred buttons. But first your gang must cut the slabs under the throne. The Abbey rehearsals Up Above must be over by now.'

'Kill Ex-Prime Minister Foot-Webb,' chanted the turncoat Rats. 'Exterminate *all* traitors to the Queen!' And they glared menacingly at the Opposition – which stood as one body, then evacuated the House in disgust.

CHAPTER FIFTEEN

Anti-Germ Warfare

In the streets Up Above, further protests and last minute demonstrations against the new Republic filled the evening before Abdication Day. Mrs Stanmore had to force her way through a group of furious women in Ebury Street who were shouting loudly to keep the Monarchy in place. They wanted her to join them, but they looked far too terrifying. They were waving their flags as if they were weapons, and their faces were unnaturally red from all the exertion. Breaking away, she was relieved to get back to the flat. She would warn Suzie not to visit Clare or venture out while the rioting was going on.

'Suzie, where *are* you?' she called through the empty rooms. Neither Jane nor Clare knew her whereabouts when she phoned them. Mrs Stanmore grew frantic.

'If she isn't back soon I must call the police. It's nasty out there. I don't want her caught up in the troubles.'

Suzie lay rigid with fear in the Inspection Chamber where she had been flung. She was curled up tight in a bedraggled ball, so scared she could barely breathe. When she had been dragged past Pompey earlier and flung into the cooler, the gigantic beast, dozing contentedly after his meal, had momentarily opened his watery yellow eyes to gaze upon her, and had munched his jaws together, grunting. Next, she had been alarmed by the crashing manhole covers that announced Parliament at nine. Now she was far too wretched and hungry to think of sleep.

She listened to the guards pace up and down the Tumbling Bay outside, their scaly feet scratching the ground. Then she tried to work out why the Prime Minister had acted the way he did. His betrayal had been so shocking because their friendship, she was sure, had been real. It was all very puzzling. How could Harold Foot-Webb have used her like that just to get the Princess for himself? Then she remembered that people do strange things when they fall in love. Look at what happened to Dad . . . he'd altered completely. It was as if she and Mum hadn't existed for him any more.

As she eventually sobbed herself to sleep, Suzie decided quite firmly that *she* would never fall in love.

Some time later, bristling whiskers brushed her cheek and tickled her awake. A low growly voice said, 'Keep absolutely quiet!'

Suzie would have screamed – because it was the hairy face of Igor the Rat only inches away – but a slimy webbed hand was placed firmly over her mouth. It felt like being kissed by a frog.

'Sshh! Silent as a soil-pipe. Listen carefully.'

A great spotted face loomed close, its plug-ugly features glistening with slime.

'Princess Griselda!'

'We've come to rescue you. But we can't talk here. I know a safe place under the French Embassy.'

'But what about the guards? How did you get past?'

'I sent them away with a bribe. I gave them some buttons I unpicked off the train of my wedding gown. Plus my second helping of shepherd's pie. I didn't eat it in case I got too fat for my dress.'

As she spoke, Suzie noticed that Princess

Griselda had changed. Her voice had grown serious and urgent. Her face, too, was full of concern.

'Hurry!' growled Igor. 'They'll be back. They must go on guarding this empty cell thinking you're still inside. By the time they find out, you'll have vanished completely. Follow closely. The Princess will lead.'

Suzie dared not use her torch, so in the darkness there was nothing for it but to hold on to Igor's ropy tail. Once away from the Palace, Suzie switched on her light, and they reached the French Embassy at a terrific pace. Suzie remembered to stand well back from the Embassy outlet, just in case she was deluged by perfumed foam. There was no knowing when the French might bathe.

'Now listen,' said Princess Griselda. 'I've watched at close quarters while my mother has slowly gone mad. Right now, my Harold is trying to win the vote in Parliament to prevent my mother's wretched plot. If he wins, she'll rave and condemn him to death. If he loses, she'll still be after him. Either way, Harold is in mortal danger. *You* must help save him.'

'Save him! He wanted me eaten!'

'Listen hard, Suzie. I *know* that Harold is the only one who can hold the sewer together. He must marry me and rule. Mother still treats me like a child – she's made every decision for me. I've been stifled. But marrying Harold is the one thing I really want. You *have* to help save him.'

Suzie looked sullen and hung her head. But Griselda wasn't having this. 'This is really urgent. I want you to go to the Sauna Baths, Suzie. Help him get an army together, one that's strong and brave enough to storm the Palace. If the Sludge-Gulpers' vote has been defeated, they'll be feeling useless and desperate. They'll need you to rally them. I'll stay here at the Palace – ready to let you all in – and await my Squidgy, who has promised to come and claim me for his bride, whatever happens. Sir Bounders Green will be trying his hardest to prevent this. If you fail, I'll be forced to stay with that wretch for ever. Go quickly – Igor will guard you. Now is the time to travel. Everyone's been rounded up to vote – you won't meet a soul. I'll return to the Palace and pretend to be asleep before Mother comes back. She *must* think I'm on her side.'

Suzie considered all this for a moment. But she remained adamant. 'I'm sorry, but I refuse to help. I won't do a thing more for Harold Foot-Webb. I no longer trust him. He wanted me eaten!'

'Idiot One-Off!' said the Princess angrily.

'Don't you realize he *pretended* to side with the Queen? She could easily have had you fed to Pompey. Harold got you thrown in here to give us time to rescue you.'

'Quick march!' Igor commanded, nipping Suzie slightly to start her on her way.

For most of the journey Suzie was silent. She was too tired and confused to work things out. She dreamed of her mother's casserole, full of different vegetables, all creamy and hot. This made her feel better. Then she remembered something. Wasn't it from the Sauna Baths that you could go through the special door to get to the disused platform at Covent Garden? Suzie could mysteriously disappear, take the tube back home, and be just in time to eat an enormous meal. Her mother would be waiting with outstretched arms.

As Griselda had predicted, the sewers were deserted, and they reached the Sauna Baths without incident. There, the large black Rat left Suzie alone, saying he would return to the Palace to protect the Princess.

At first Suzie was not allowed in. An unfamiliar guard had been posted outside, and she did not know the password. But when Jacusi appeared and saw who it was, she grabbed her arm and pulled her through the steam into the Inspection Chamber.

'Suzie! Thank 'eavens! We thought you might've been killed. They'll be mighty pleased to see you. They need 'elp – real bad.'

A dejected company of Sludge-Gulpers and friendly Rats crouched slumped and exhausted all round the secret meeting place. Harold Foot-Webb was not there.

'He's left us. He disappeared with a secret plan we do not know about,' explained Rickman-sworthy.

'Gone bravely off on his own for help, he says,' croaked Frogmorton.

'Probably discharged himself to live in exile, before he gets caught,' suggested Angel Rat.

But when the Parliamentary fiasco was described to Suzie and she heard how Harold Foot-Webb had spoken up so courageously, she refused to believe that Angel Rat's theory was true. Griselda had been right all the time. And here they were, all wretched and confused . . . and without their leader to guide them.

'We've only just this minute made it back,' growled Shadwell gruffly, 'and it was a fur-raising experience, I can tell you. We were scampering for our lives!'

'We had to scarper, sharpish,' Chigwell explained, 'because we heard the Slime-

Grubbers threatening to get an army together to destroy everybody who voted on the side of Ex-Prime Minister Foot-Webb. Now we haven't the soggiest what to do. We'll have to defend ourselves somehow.'

'The Queen wants all traitors caught by tomorrow,' said Edna. 'Pompey's been promised an enormous Wedding Day feast!'

'This is the worst calamity that's ever happened in Sir Bazalgette's kingdom,' pronounced Purley, miserably curling his toes. 'He'd be devastated to know that the place he built for us has gone to rack and ruin.'

As Suzie listened, and saw their downcast faces, so tired and dejected, a strange feeling welled up inside her, making her grow hot, making her heart beat urgently. She took some short, hard breaths, then found herself leaping on to the platform like a practised Sludge-Gulper.

'We'll do more than defend ourselves! *We will attack!*' she announced. 'We'll also save my Queen from tumbling and so stop the sewer creatures being discovered. We'll chuck Queen Greenmould out of her Palace and stop the wedding taking place. *We will form an army of our own, and I will be your leader!*'

Something very peculiar had happened to Suzie. All thoughts of escape had left her mind.

139

Now it was as if a new Suzie had stepped out of the old. The new Suzie was strong and unafraid.

'Is the Acro-prop still where we left it?' she wanted to know.

'The prop is where we left it, camouflaged with sludge,' confirmed Frogmorton.

'Then this is what we'll do. A small group will go and get the prop. This will include me as I must explain how it works and make sure it's positioned properly under the throne. The rest of you must assemble an army and meet us under the Abbey to guard the prop until the Queen Up Above is safe. Then we'll march straight to the Palace to capture the Queen and stop Sir Bounders Green marrying the Princess. *But . . .* our army has to be strong and have a clever strategy, if it's to overcome Queen Greenmould.'

'Her army will be much bigger than ours,' squealed Shadwell.

'Then we must think of some brilliant ideas,' Suzie insisted. 'The Prime Minister was good at logic – maybe the rest of you are, too? You Rats say you are clever – well, this is the time to use cunning. Think everybody, *think*.'

And Suzie's enthusiasm worked. The depression lifted, the meeting jumped into action. Everyone was prepared to use logic, algebra, maths – whatever would help. Suggestions were made about separating the enemy into small pockets, then fighting them. Another idea was to make a surprise attack – perhaps an ambush of some kind. None quite had the core of brilliance that Suzie knew would bring certain victory.

'We need more troops, but we probably can't get them in time. So what we need is some kind of weapon. Isn't there something they're scared of?' she asked.

'Yes, Humans,' laughed Angel Rat, sarcastically.

'No, I mean some weapon we could use against them that they detest. What do Slime-Grubbers and Rats *really hate*?'

'Distant fectant,' yelled Steaming Lil.

'And bleach,' shouted Jucusi. 'They can't abide that, neither.'

'By the Works at Beckton! I think you've got something there!' exclaimed Rickmansworthy. 'Well done! Excellent logic. What you're talking about is a kind of Anti-Germ Warfare.'

'That's exactly it!' Suzie was jubilant. 'Anti-Germ Warfare.'

'The Fluffers've got distant fectant and bleach. I know they 'ave,' called Steaming Lil. 'We could filch some.'

'A Fluffer? What's a Fluffer?' Suzie asked.

'Bless me, don't you know?' Edna smiled.

141

'Fluffers are the ladies that clean the platforms, after the last tube's gone.'

'I know where their supplies is kept,' divulged Steaming Lil.

'So do I,' Jacusi chuckled. 'In them lockers at the far end of Platform 2. Where do you think I get all me mops and buckets?'

'Then I'll go and get some,' Suzie volunteered. 'And some J-Cloths to act as masks so we don't get disinfected ourselves.'

'We'll dip the mops in distant fectant and *advance*!' yelled Steaming Lil, doing a dance with Edna.

'We'll get some liquid bleach and *squirt* 'em!' shrieked Jacusi.

'Bless us all,' croaked Granny Gulper. 'Then everythin'll be all right.'

While the troops were being strengthened with massive helpings of revolting Southwark stew from Steaming Lil's cauldron, Suzie chose this delicate moment to ask Rickmansworthy for some cash. Then she found and happily raided the machines on platform 2 for fizzy drinks and chocolate – not only to avoid Southwark stew, but as an excuse to look around. She found the lockers. There were four of them, with names chalked on: Esme, Tonia, Maureen and Anna.

They were all unlocked. 'But then,' Suzie thought, 'who would *want* to steal disinfectant and bleach?'

It was now very late. Trains were running few and far between. It was not difficult for Suzie to empty every locker. Soon she had enough ammunition for a whole army.

As Big Ben chimed midnight and the city fell silent, Suzie was back in the Inspection Chamber with her troops, making plans for a combined outfit of Sludge-Gulpers and Rats that would go down in sewer history as 'Operation Royal Flush'.

CHAPTER SIXTEEN

Pig Without Porkfolio

Underneath Westminster Abbey and the Houses of Parliament lives an ancient order of Grey Rats. It is a sacred sect that can trace its history back to the days of Edward the Confessor. The Grey Rat is small, because it lives entirely on a diet of the meagre left-overs from the Parliamentary canteens Up Above. The ancient Ratacombs where the Grey Rats dwell twist and weave about in a tiny area, built and rebuilt over countless years since medieval times. As these tunnels are smaller than the average sewer, many are no longer used, and sometimes pockets of foul gas can get trapped. It is said that were a Human to walk into one by mistake, it would drop as if hit with a length of lead piping.

Harold Foot-Webb made his way towards the Abbey, plunging straight from the House of

Lords northwards towards the Ratacombs, with no thought in his head except to look for help. Before long he was utterly lost.

Confused and exhausted, eventually he stopped, lay down on the dry earth of a disused tunnel, and closed his eyes to ponder what to do next. This foolish idea was completely against his nature. Logic was not in it, nor, he realized, was common sense. He had chosen to embark on this worm-brained scheme to save his friends . . . and he had already fouled it up. Time was running out.

When he opened his eyes, a Grey Rat stood motionless on its back legs, looking down at him. Bravely, the Sludge-Gulper poured out his story to the Rat. Then, Ignatius, head of the sacred rats – for he it was – asked the Ex-Prime Minister to follow him and meet his Company.

Grey Rats are a quiet lot, pacifist and neutral when it comes to politics. (It is said they got that way from hearing all the noisy debates in Parliament Up Above.) However, Ignatius had picked up various squeaks and rumours from several of his Rats who had been disturbed by the rowdiness in the Sewer House of Commons, and was extremely troubled to hear of the Queen's outrageous plan. His Rats promised to help in every way they could. First, the Sludge-Gulper was escorted safely back to under

Parliament Square, then an emergency meeting of Grey Rats was called. One after another, they filed into an old empty boiler which they said concentrated the mind. In Ignatius's Think-Tank, intelligent plans were laid.

While the Think-Tank was at work, so were Sir Bounders Green and his slime-grubbing gang. They had waited ages in a stinking mood for the Abbey to be clear. Something was always going on: washing, polishing, decorating – then an extensive choir practice. At midnight, when all the Humans had finally gone home, they could at last start. They carefully cut – almost – through the grouting which secured the marble slabs, then braced them, just sufficiently, beneath. It was a difficult task.

Queen Greenmould had returned triumphant from Parliament to Palace. Her Slime-Grubbers were booby-trapping the throne, the 'sacrifice' who would receive the blame for Operation Royal Regalia was waiting in the cooler ready to go into the net – everything was going according to plan. First she would instruct Lady Loo to train her newly titled Rats to form a great Pulling Team to haul the booty away. Next she would get an army assembled to capture every creature in the Sauna Baths, and then feed them to Pompey. Soon the complete London Sewer system would be hers, to rule over *for ever*.

As they turned into the main gate and were greeted by a sleepy grunt from Pompey, a squeal of anguish erupted from the Pig Without Porkfolio. Outside the Inspection Chamber was an upturned corgi bowl. The door was swinging open; the cooler was deserted; the guards had disappeared completely. The Queen howled when she found her Hand-Maiden gone. She clenched her webbed fingers into tight knots, then uncurled one finger, pointed it at her Pig, and shouted:

'For your first new job, Sir Pig Without Porkfolio, I command you to recapture that Human before the Abdication Ceremony begins. *With your snout, search her out!*'

At the Sauna Baths, Suzie prepared to set out to get the Acro-prop. A small gang, consisting of Purley, Rickmansworthy and Frogmorton, had elected to go with her. Those left behind would assemble and train the troops. Shadwell would drill the Rats; Edna, the Sludge-Gulpers. Many more Rats loyal to their cause were needed. Every Sludge-Gulper available also had to be rounded up. When a large enough army was gathered and given Anti-Germ weapons, it would follow Suzie's gang to protect the Acro once this was in place.

'Good luck! Go carefully,' warned Chigwell. 'Patrols will be posted at every entrance round the Abbey. Others will be on the look-out to capture Harold Foot-Webb.'

'And me – once they find I've escaped,' added Suzie.

'Then a J-Cloth will help you to be disguised, as well as stop you being affected by your own Anti-Germ Warfare,' said Jacusi, tying one firmly over Suzie's nose. 'We'll all wear 'em. There!'

'Jumpin' J-Cloths, Suzie!' shrieked Steaming Lil. 'You don't 'arf look a fright!'

Equipped and ready, the gang departed, taking a couple of disinfected mops to help attack the Slime-Grubbers they knew would be guarding the booby trap. Quietly and carefully they travelled, alert and ready to fight anyone who tried to stop them.

Several times they heard patrols come near, and quickly dodged into the first side entrance they could find, until the danger passed. But to their surprise, the sewers were strangely deserted.

'Maybe the whole lot's been rounded up for the Queen's army,' Purley remarked. 'It's all very strange.'

They reached the tributary where the Acro-prop waited. The exact place was easily identified by Miss Arabella Finchley's flexible card. Inside the entrance, Suzie's torch picked out a dark shape. She jumped back in alarm and got ready to charge it with her mop. Then a face looked up, lit up, and leapt over.

'By Bazalgette! Suzie, you managed to escape!'

'And you haven't been caught by the Slime-Grubbers, Harold Foot-Webb!'

'Please forgive me for getting you flung in the Inspection Chamber.'

'Of course I do. I know now it was to save my life.'

They clenched hands so tightly that hers shot from his like a soapy balloon. Suzie smiled, realising how fond of this creature she had become.

'Let's get flowing,' urged Rickmansworthy. 'If we talk, it must be in whispers, and we should travel as fast as we can. It's not very far to go, but we can't afford to be seen with the Acro.'

Harold Foot-Webb was J-Clothed. Then, with teamwork efficiency, the Sludge-Gulpers extracted the prop, wiped off the excess sludge, and hoisted it on to their shoulders. Suzie led the way, holding the mops and torch. As they travelled, Suzie told Harold Foot-Webb about the army. He was much impressed with the Anti-Germ Warfare logic.

'A good, watertight plan. Well done!'

In turn, he described his meeting with the Company of Grey Rats.

'They are on our side, so you need not be afraid. They're not allowed to fight, but they've promised to help. To get to the Abbey we have to pass under Parliament, but the Grey Rats have offered to wait at the entrance to the Rata-combs to show us a secret way which should avoid the Queen's patrols.'

When they reached Parliament, Purley whispered, 'Quiet! Look! There's a patrol of Slime-Grubbers guarding the sewer entrance.'

'Yes, I can see five of them!' whispered Harold Foot-Webb. 'Put down the prop carefully. Let's creep nearer, two of us coming from each side.'

As quiet as mice they separated and inched closer. Then, at Frogmorton's signal, each side charged, shouting wildly, whirling their mops and spraying disinfectant in every direction. The astonished guards screeched with shock and fled. Two smarter ones rushed back towards the Palace to inform the Queen that some very strange creatures were around.

The Prop Gang's strategy worked better than they could ever have imagined. Under Parliament they travelled until Harold Foot-Webb turned them north at the first junction they came to. He explained that although the Abbey was not very far away Up Above, the sewers below were exceedingly twisty and complex as they were some of the oldest in London. The small sewer he chose was indeed very strange. Its brickwork was cracked and slippery, and the atmosphere was so warm and damp that mushrooms hung like giant icicles from the roof – some greasy and white, others pointed and black. The puddles that covered the floor were filled with small, anaemic-looking worms.

'Perhaps we're under the Houses of Parliament central heating boiler,' Rickmansworthy suggested. 'Oh dear, where do we go now?'

'Follow me. This disused sewer eventually leads to the Ratacombs entrance,' Harold Foot-Webb encouraged them. 'Just carry on. I know the way.'

The tunnel wound along, becoming so turgid and dry that their own disinfectant fumes were trapped. It managed to penetrate the J-Cloths. The Sludge-Gulpers found the stuff most offensive. They coughed and spluttered as harsh vapours struck their throats. Eyes streamed, making it hard to see. It felt, too, as if they had travelled in a circle. Suzie was getting so tired that when a wide, deserted chamber came to her rescue, she begged them to stop for a rest. Stalactites hung, ghostly-white, from a high-arched roof, while below, the sewage slowed to a thick, limpid pool, full of decomposed matter, which made the air around them stagnant and foul.

'This is it – the entrance to the Ratacombs, the high security zone under the protection of the Sacred Grey Rats!' cried Harold Foot-Webb.

'Yes, but they are *not* here to greet us,' Purley panicked.

They rested the great prop on the sludge. Everything was so still and quiet that they felt increasingly uneasy. They waited. No Grey Rats appeared. Harold Foot-Webb was filled with despair. His followers would think he had let them down. They wouldn't trust him ever again.

'They did promise,' he said in a quiet voice, as the other creatures found they could no longer look at him. 'Maybe something prevented them from being here.'

Suzie could not bear this situation. She got up to investigate with her torch. More than ten or twelve small entrances, all in various stages of disrepair, lay directly ahead. The older, more decrepit outlets were on a higher level, many blocked with dry earthy deposits. Others were as soft as gingerbread – you could have scooped them out with a teaspoon. Suddenly Suzie noticed some strange markings on the ground.

'Hey! Look! There are some little footprints

in the mud going along this tunnel. They seem quite recent.'

'Those can only be the hoof-marks of the Pig,' said Harold Foot-Webb, who had quickly leapt over. '*That's* perhaps why there were no Grey Rats to meet us. And *that's* the tunnel we'll take,' he announced. 'Come on.'

They had only wormed their way round the first bend, when they were stopped by a high-pitched squeal. There *was* the Swamp Pig, blocking their way.

'Blithering bung-holes! You were quite right, Prime Minister, the Swamp Pig must have terrified the Rats!' swore Frogmorton.

The disinfectant had no effect on the Pig at all. He thrust his hoofs into the mud and stood his ground, glaring from piercing pink eyes.

'Stay exactly where you are – and you, spy! I know it's you from the green wellington boots. Once I succeeded in scaring off those stupid Grey Rats, I knew I'd be able to claim the Queen's reward.'

'Out of my way, Swamp Pig!' commanded Harold Foot-Webb.

'You don't fool me either, Un-Prime Minister. I no longer have to do as *you* say,' snorted the Pig. 'You forget, I'm Pig Without Porkfolio now and you should address me as Sir.'

'Pig Without Pigment, more like,' taunted Harold Foot-Webb.

The Pig smashed his front hoofs down and snorted. 'My mistress the Queen will hear of this. You'll not get far. I can go through these tunnels faster than any of you – and I'm already on my way to alert her.'

With that, the little Pig turned and trotted off.

'After him!' shouted Rickmansworthy. 'Let's fight him.'

But Suzie held him back.

'Stop Pig!' she yelled with all her might.

The Pig stopped dead in his tracks and faced Suzie. There was something in that yell that made his blood run cold.

'*You stupid Pig!* Don't you know what *roast pork* means?'

The Swamp Pig stared.

'What *is* roast pork?' he asked in a quiet voice. 'They keep mentioning it in front of me, then they laugh.'

'Roast pork is little Pig, usually chopped into nice juicy joints, smeared with a little lard, then *roasted*,' said Suzie, emphatically. 'Don't you realize that your "mistress", as you call her, and the whole Royal Court, intend to *eat* you in a few hours' time for the Wedding Breakfast?'

The small Pig winced. His piggy eyes stared in disbelief. Then, all of a sudden, he understood. He let out so long and lamenting a squeal that its echo seemed to last for ever.

After that Sir Pig Without Porkfolio altered. He looked smaller, more vulnerable, appearing to tremble. He opened his snout to grunt, but nothing came out.

And Suzie, filled with pity, waded up to pat him on the head.

'There, there, little Pig. We'll take care of you.'

So the little Pig joined their ranks – and it was a good thing that he did, because he was the only one who knew the way.

CHAPTER SEVENTEEN

Snap! Snap! Snap!

It was the dead of night when Sir Pig Without Porkfolio guided the Prop Gang unerringly through the maze of tunnels that led to the Abbey. Harold Foot-Webb explained the plans to the Pig. In return, he told them all he knew.

'The booby trap is set,' said the Pig. 'The biggest problem now is the Alligator. The Queen has left him to guard it.'

'The Alligator? Oh no!' exclaimed Frogmorton.

The Prop Gang stopped, looking utterly dismayed. After all the effort of getting the prop this far, they wouldn't be able to use it, because of Pompey.

'You see, the Queen knew that you would form an army against her. So she's put Sir Kenzal Green and the Duke of Dalston in charge of rounding up practically every creature left in the

Sewers so that her troops will outnumber yours ten to one.'

'So that's why the sewers are virtually deserted,' said Purley.

'They're all being organized and drilled at this very moment, so Pompey's been positioned beneath the throne until a guarding squad can be spared. They've fixed him on to a long chain, and deliberately allowed him to bellow to keep intruders away. But he's furious about being moved, and has worked himself into quite a lather.'

'What if they hear him during the Abdication ceremony?' asked Suzie.

'The Queen thinks she'll be able to replace him with *you* long before that!' said the Swamp Pig.

'What do you mean?' Suzie stopped short. Her face had drained as white as a sewer mushroom.

'You'll have to know sooner or later. The Queen is raging mad that you've escaped. She had planned to dangle you underneath the throne, so that when your Queen fell through, you would be the one blamed by Up Above for trying to kill her.'

'But . . . but they'll accuse me of . . . what is it called when you kill a queen – regicide!' Suzie was aghast. She knew from history that regicide meant being rowed through Traitor's Gate into the Tower of London to have your head chopped off. But today, if anything, it would be worse. If she told them about the 'weird sewer creatures', they'd lock her in a mental asylum, maybe sedate her with pills for life. Suddenly she wanted very much to go back home.

'We'll not let it happen!' Purley promised, trying to comfort her.

'By Bazalgette, I'll protect you!' swore Harold Foot-Webb.

'That won't be possible, Prime Minister,' insisted the Pig. 'Not with the sumptuous reward of five hundred buttons put out for your capture.'

For several moments there was a horrified silence. Then the musty air was blown apart by an angry bellow very close at hand.

'Ssh! Quiet as a blockage! He's just around the corner,' warned the Pig. 'We can't possibly get past him if we take this route. However, there is a narrow medieval sewer that skirts around to the other side of Pompey. It's deep in Sacred Territory, but I know the way. Follow me.'

They were about to set off when Purley heard a slight clanking, and signalled the others to stop. He had noticed the very end of a chain, hooked through a strong iron rung. Where the chain met the ground was a large amount of slack before it disappeared out of sight.

'I think I'm on to something here!' he whispered. 'Try to help!'

He crept over to the chain, unhooked it, and gesturing to the others, showed them what each must do. Nodding their understanding, they picked up the slack chain ever so gently . . . knowing that at any moment they might alert the beast on the other end of it, which would come hurtling back to kill them. Then they held it while Purley tenderly hooked it back on the rung much further along, making the chain almost taut. He had shortened it considerably. Then they crept back to take the Pig's route round the throne.

It was the narrowest sewer yet. They had to squeeze along, with Suzie bending her head uncomfortably. In several areas the brickwork had crumbled, blocking some smaller outlets completely. 'We must be under the very heart of the Abbey now,' she thought. All at once, she felt the enormous weight of the place pressing down on her: the ancient marble slabs upon which rested carved Ladies and their Knights, the heavy font, the massive columns that supported the nave. She shuddered and tried to travel faster. Once or twice she was aware of grey shadows whisking away from them just ahead, and knew they were being watched.

But the Swamp Pig persevered. Occasionally

the air was filled with Pompey's blasts getting louder and nearer. Before long their tunnel enlarged, then joined the sewer the other side of Pompey. Round the next bend they could hear grunting, and the clanking of his chain.

'We're there!' whispered the Pig. 'Let's see if your scheme has worked, Purley.'

He let out a small, tentative squeal. At once this was answered by an angry bellow. The gang crept round the bend to find themselves in a high, vaulted chamber with Pompey in the middle. The gigantic, horrifying beast was straining for all he was worth towards them. His scaly legs heaved sideways, each lifted in turn as it scraped along the floor to grip the mud. His chain, however, ended several feet short of the strange apparatus hanging from the roof, which they knew at once was Greenmould's booby trap.

'Well done, Purley!' cried Suzie.

'Brilliant logic!' the others congratulated him.

With the furious beast slavering and snapping, they inched nearer, still fearful that he might be able to wrench himself free. Suzie looked above her. The trap was some distance beyond her reach. It had been made with great precision: a neat, flat lattice of rods, expertly woven, spread the load of what she knew was Edward I's heavy wooden throne, positioned directly above. The trap seemed perfect: strong enough to support the weight of the throne . . . until somebody Up Above sat down. A fisherman's net was hanging below, ready to catch the Queen. A couple of spare drain-rods had been left on the ground. A Union Jack – obviously stolen from the Abbey – had been made into a lumpy bag which swayed gently from the vibrations of Pompey's bellowing. Suzie shivered. 'That's where they wanted to leave me.'

Rickmansworthy was getting very nervous.

'Let's get to work,' he shouted above the noise. 'We don't want him to break his chain with rage.' And he began to dismantle the net.

Now the bellowing built up into a roaring crescendo of permanent echoes which chilled them to the core. Above this racket Suzie tried to explain – mostly in sign language – how they would place the Acro-prop under the lattice of rods to take the full weight of the throne. Then, while one of them shone the torch, she would take the holding-pin from the ratchet, wind the prop tight against the lattice, and replace the pin at a higher level to hold the prop in place.

Pompey started to make small runs at them, his clanking chain choking him just out of reach while he snatched viciously towards them. In this nerve-shattering situation, they started to haul the prop. But when they held it against the lattice and tried to lengthen it, the ratchets wouldn't budge.

'They must have rusted in the sludge! What can we do?' Suzie was at her wit's end. Pompey was getting angrier and angrier. Saliva dripped continually from between his glistening teeth and formed a foaming puddle on the floor.

'Never fear!' shouted Rickmansworthy. Then he and the other Sludge-Gulpers proceeded to smear a little of their slime over the ratchets and other moving parts to ease them. In no time at all, the prop was winched tightly in place, pressing hard against the lattice. Last of all, the pin was replaced to secure the whole thing. If it could hold up a ceiling it could hold up a wooden throne. Then all of a sudden Pompey stopped bellowing. A grunt of pleasure followed. Excited voices – and footsteps – were coming their way.

What happened next was a nightmare. Queen Greenmould and Lady Loo rounded the corner. They were accompanied by Sir Bounders Green and the Honourable Harry Neasden, who wanted Her Majesty to inspect their work. Suzie and the others were trapped between the jaws of Pompey on one side, and the inspection party on the other. There was no escape.

When the Queen saw her booby trap sabotaged, and their prop in place, she let out a ghastly shriek. With eyes bulging in hate, she heaved towards them like a huge rolling lump of lard.

'You filthy sump-mucus! You slime-moulds! You dung-maggots!'

'Protect the prop!' yelled Rickmansworthy.

'Overpower them!' called Harold Foot-Webb. He grabbed a drain-rod and made for the Queen. Frogmorton made for the other spare rod, but the Queen had plunged towards it. Then it was in her hand as she lashed out furiously at their handiwork, smashing at it wildly. Next, she turned on Rickmansworthy with several accurate blows. Her enormous bulk seemed to be everywhere at once. Frogmorton threw his heavy body at Sir Bounders Green and Harry Neasden, attempting to bowl them over. For a few moments Suzie was terrified stupid. Then she jumped into action. Grabbing the disinfected mop, she set about Lady Loo, jabbing and swiping.

'Get back, Spy! Traitor! Scumbag!' jeered Lady Loo.

'Get back yourself, stink-pipe! Warty toad!' challenged Suzie, flashing her torch in her opponent's face, then disinfecting her so that she gurgled.

The Queen now lunged at Harold Foot-Webb, whilst Purley began to belabour her fat body

163

from behind. But her 'spare tyres' were as rubbery as real tyres, and his thumping had no effect. Even Harold Foot-Webb's drain-rod kept bouncing off. She threw herself forward, swamping him in her folds.

'Stand back!' squealed the little Pig. 'Leave this luxury to me!'

In an unbridled rage, the Pig Without Porkfolio flung himself at the Queen's legs, and munched at her toes in revenge.

'Oooh! Aaaagh!' The Queen was on her feet in an instant, hopping painfully. 'Pig, how *dare* you!' she yelped . . . before the look in his eyes told her that *now*, perhaps, he knew about Roast Pork.

'Retreat!' gurgled Lady Loo, pulling the Queen away.

Frogmorton had Harry Neasden flattened, Sir Bounders Green was being punished unmercifully by Rickmansworthy, Purley was ready to make another charge, and the Pig was about to launch a second munching attack. Even the Alligator was snapping indiscriminately at anyone who came too close.

'Not yet, Lady Loo. Wait! I have a very simple way to finish them off all in one!' Leering horribly, Greenmould threw herself past Pompey and disappeared round the bend. Then they heard her undoing Pompey's chain. With the monster about to be set free, Frogmorton, Rickmansworthy and Purley rushed off as fast as they could. Suzie, the Pig and Harold Foot-Webb, still clutching his drain-rod, followed.

'Crunch them, Pompey! Gobble them up!' she yelled . . . and was about to let her Alligator go, when, in a stroke of genius, she had a further stupendous idea.

'Hold on, Pompey! Not *just* yet!' Quickly she wound his chain twice round the Acro-prop and held tight to the other end. 'After them, Pompey! Pull! *Now!*' she yelled, giving him a terrific thwack with her loo brush.

The great beast lurched off to do his mistress's bidding.

Suzie turned – and screamed. For an instant the others stopped and gaped. The great beast had wrenched the prop sideways, causing it to stick at a precarious angle. Then the Queen let her Alligator go. So fast did he charge away that he knocked the Queen flying. Then he was off on the chase after them, his scaly legs pushing sideways, his massive jaws crashing open and shut: *Snap! Snap! Snap!*

CHAPTER EIGHTEEN

The Sluice-Gate

However hard they ran, whichever way they turned, they could hear the bellowing Alligator getting close. Frogmorton, Rickmansworthy and Purley were way in front. Then came the Pig, squealing fit to burst. Then Suzie, flashing her torch from one side of the tunnel to the other, hurtling along as fast as her wellingtons would allow. Behind them, Harold Foot-Webb was the nearest to Pompey's bone-crunching jaws with their gruesome teeth.

'Stop!' he yelled. 'I've got an idea!'

Suzie and the Swamp Pig did stop – dead in their tracks – and stared. Harold Foot-Webb had turned to face Pompey. Had he gone crazy?

'Come on, Prime Minister! What are you doing? He'll kill you!'

Thrashing his tail with pleasure, Pompey approached his prey. He'd never eaten Sludge-

Gulper, this one looked most juicy and plump – very rubbery indeed! He put on more speed and opened his massive jaws. Harold Foot-Webb waited, backed a little, carefully positioned the drain-rod he was still carrying, and then, when he saw the craggy mouth gape at its widest, he forced the drain-rod in, prising the top and bottom jaws apart.

The surprised animal tried to shut his jaws, but couldn't – nor could he open them further.

Suzie screamed and backed away. Harold Foot-Webb, his heroic deed accomplished, tried to press himself against the sewer wall, avoiding the reach of the startled beast thrashing wildly from one side of the tunnel to the other. The terrified Pig rushed this way and that to avoid his whipping tail.

Try as he might to worry the drain-rod away, the Alligator's great body swung uselessly and only succeeded in tearing its beautifully polished scales.

Then, quite suddenly, the Alligator gave up. The struggling stopped. It stumbled to a halt and groaned, turning helplessly towards Suzie. A strange gurgling had started at the back of its throat.

Suzie thought, 'Is it about to die?' Gradually she crept nearer. To her surprise, fat tears welled in Pompey's eyes and poured steadily down.

'He's crying!' she exclaimed. 'Are they only crocodile tears, though?' she wondered. 'Is he just pretending, so he can snap me up?'

But Pompey was a piteous sight. His whole body heaved with sobs – and they were real enough for Suzie. She moved even nearer. Still he didn't show any signs of attacking her.

'Don't,' she begged. 'Please don't cry.' She couldn't bear it. All his fierceness had left him. It was as if that scaly armour of his had been stripped away to reveal a gentle creature, hiding inside.

'I'll help you,' she said reassuringly. She was so close that she could see the yellow of his eyes. Then she looked right into his eyes – and saw such a sad, hopeless expression there, that suddenly she knew exactly what to do. Grasping her torch in both hands, she swung it sideways and, with all her might, smashed the drain-rod from his jaws.

'What are you *doing*?' cried Harold Foot-Webb.

'We're done for now!' squealed the Pig, calling for Frogmorton, Purley and Rickmansworthy to help – but they were miles ahead, way out of sight. Just the three of them were left to ward off the beast.

'Poor Alligator, you were flushed down just like the Pig. It's not your fault you were captured by the Queen. You've been brainwashed, never known any other life, never had a chance.'

Pompey stopped crying. This was the only creature who had ever talked to him like this. From somewhere through his suffering he started to think for himself for the very first time. He began to speak, but the words came out with great difficulty.

'The Queen forced me to guard the Palace, chained me to the wall. All I've ever had to do is keep other creatures away, frighten them almost to death . . . bellow and bellow and bellow.'

'And what would you prefer to do instead?'

'To do . . . whatever alligators are supposed to do. I really don't know. Swim, perhaps? Hunt, perhaps?'

'Then from now on, you'll be *free!*' Suzie pronounced. 'You'll never be tied up again. Here's what you've got to do. Follow every sewer travelling downstream. Eventually you'll come to the River Thames. Make your way into the water, and then swim downstream into the estuary . . . away to the sea.'

Pompey's eyes glistened. 'Free! Free!' he bellowed, gathering more and more speed as he rushed off down the tunnel. Soon he had disappeared, swallowed by the gloom.

The other two stared at Suzie in amazement

and admiration. Suzie herself was exhilarated. She also felt light and different – as though, by freeing Pompey, she had started to unravel that hard knot inside her own head. Now, she felt strong and brave. She would be able to cope with any difficulty that lay ahead.

When the last bellow had faded away, the remains of the Prop Gang took stock of their situation.

'I think we must be lost, and the other three are miles ahead,' sighed Harold Foot-Webb.

Even the Swamp Pig was confused about where they were, after the chase.

'Let's get back to the prop,' Harold Foot-Webb decided. 'Our army must have set out by now, and that is where they are headed.'

'The only good thing about this is that the Queen will think we've been eaten, and won't expect us back,' reasoned Suzie.

They began to retrace their steps, but found themselves walking more and more slowly – they were all terribly tired.

Then a long, cold draught blew straight into their faces, followed almost immediately by a hollow rumbling. Suzie thought it was a train.

'Rain!' shouted Harold Foot-Webb. 'It's rain. Hurry! We've got to get to a higher outlet – or we could drown.'

'But it can't be rain,' cried Suzie. 'They said on telly that tomorrow was going to be fine.'

'It can't be anything else,' the Pig insisted. 'That sound is unmistakable. There must've been a sudden storm Up Above. We've got to find an Expansion Chamber before it's too late.'

Already the water level was rising, and there was the sound of a great wave whooshing through the tunnel behind. Panic-stricken, they charged along. Suzie clutched furiously at the little Pig. No Expansion Chamber arrived, and the tumbling deluge crashed louder, filling the tunnel completely. Then it was overhead, engulfing them like a wave sweeping in from the ocean. Water covered Suzie's face, swirled into her eyes, her nose, her mouth. The torch was dashed from her grasp, and she found herself clinging to the Pig's curly tail while he swam along. The roaring filled her head, then started to muddle her mind. She was gasping, and could no longer breathe. They were shooting through the sewer with amazing speed.

In a spinning vortex Suzie whirled. The blackness was like a blanket, enfolding her. She felt as if she was being drawn backwards through a dream. The swirling in her head changed to a fizzing, then silence. Through the silence, strange visions floated from dark places deep in her mind. She saw her father teaching her to

171

ride her bike when she was small, then her mother saying, 'Well done, Suzie! I can hardly believe it, you being top in composition *and* maths!' Next she saw the Queen's golden coach flash past, with the Queen waving inside: 'Goodbye to you all . . . Goodbye!'

There was a jolt. They had hit a metal gate. Suzie had surfaced, and was clinging to the barrier with all her remaining strength. She opened her eyes and was dimly aware of Harold Foot-Webb above, hauling the Pig from the cascading falls up some iron rungs to a sluice-gate.

'Come on, Suzie,' he shouted – but his voice seemed very faint and distant. She held on, not daring to move. 'Come *on*, Suzie!' the voice ordered urgently. Everything was a tremendous effort as she heaved herself up. Drenched clothes stuck to her body, dragging her down. Her boots filled with water, pulling like ten-ton weights.

Ages later, it seemed, they were all perched safe on a shelf high above the water. Suzie coughed and gasped until she could breathe more easily. Then she huddled in a heap, shivering – oblivious to everything except the pounding noise in her head. Slowly she became aware of rows of red eyes glistening in the darkness next to her. Harold Foot-Webb was shouting, 'Move up, you lot! Give us more room!'

Then he said, 'It's all right, Suzie, they'll not

harm you, even if they are on the Queen's side. Sewer creatures are united in times like these. The flood is bound to go down soon.'

But it didn't. It got worse. The water, still churning, climbed steadily, swallowing the iron rungs one by one. As she got used to the gloom, Suzie realized that the red eyes belonged to eight large, sullen Rats, with great shaggy pelts soaked into tufts, and whiskers trembling with terror. She saw, too, that they were in some sort of high concrete Inspection Chamber, dimly lit from somewhere far above. The flood waters below were now full of froth, and surged into a whirl-pool, flinging up white strands of foam. Other creatures were trapped against the sluice – some mice, a drowned Rat, several long, curling eels, and, strangest of all, a complete set of false teeth, which seemed to chomp at the bars, as if trying to get a hold.

'Look!' squealed the Pig. 'Behind the sluice, the flood-gate is *shut*! It should be open to let the flood water drain away.'

Just then, a horde of Slime-Grubbers swept into the Chamber, swimming easily with their tails. Their sharp eyes pierced through the spray and spied the creatures on the shelf. Then they burst into shrill squeaks of joy.

'Like our little trick, do you?' they jabbered. 'The sudden storm was most convenient! All we had to do was wedge the sluice-gate shut! Where are you?' they taunted. 'We're coming to get you.' As they scaled the rungs, they snapped viciously.

All the creatures on the shelf desperately looked for escape. The large Rats bared their teeth and growled back, snarling in fury:

'Don't attack *us*! We're on *your* side, you stupid scaly Grubbers! We'll all be drowned if you don't open the flood-gate and empty the chamber. Unlike you, we cannot swim against such strong currents.'

'Then you'll just have to die for the cause!' the Slime-Grubbers shrilled. 'Some sacrifices have to be made for the Queen. You look like drowned Rats already. Tee, hee, hee!'

When the Rats realized their fate, they stiffened their claws and gnashed yellow teeth to join the defence of the shelf. Suzie managed to kick several Slime-Grubbers with her boots, so that they spun off, crashing back into the whirlpool. She recognized Sir Bounders Green and the Honourable Harry Neasden among them as they swam agilely back, returning to try again. And Suzie realized that they were actually enjoying themselves. They could easily have waited until their victims were drowned, then taken them back for their reward. But she remembered ... of course! They wanted her *alive*, to use under the throne. Maybe they were intending to drown the others, then drag her back to the Queen, along with the dead body of poor Harold Foot-Webb.

But because she was now standing, Suzie was high enough to discover the source of the light. It came from around the edges of a door right at the top of the Inspection Chamber. She noticed, too, some small rungs at the far end of the shelf, which led up to a walkway ending at the door.

'Excuse me, Rats,' she said suddenly, squeezing behind them, brushing against their dank wet fur.

As she climbed the rungs she heard, to her surprise, voices and laughter like a radio programme, coming from the other side of the door. Pushing it open, she fell forward into a small cluttered cellar with a concrete floor – right at the feet of a big, burly-looking man.

CHAPTER NINETEEN

Mr Barking, Maintenance and Security

'Well I'll be...! What the...?' said the man.

'*Help*!' gasped Suzie. 'Raise the flood-gates, or everyone will drown!'

There was no need for explanations. The man looked behind her down into the dark chamber.

'Blimey, the Royal Route will flood. Everything'll be ruined. Listen, girl, stay here. Dry yourself with that towel – you're drenched. I'll lever open the gate.'

The man grabbed some tools and a crowbar, reached for a headband fitted in front with a torch, then rushed through another door which led to the back of the sluice.

Suzie did not do as she had been told. Instead,

she grasped a large iron wrench and climbed back down to save her friends.

The whirlpool had reached them. It swirled over the shelf and now they clung frantically to the rungs beneath the walkway. A Slime-Grubber had caught hold of the little Pig's tail, and was pulling it so that he was squealing fit to burst. Sir Bounders Green and the Honourable Harry Neasden were snapping at Harold Foot-Webb to make him loosen his grip on the bottom rung.

Suzie smashed at the nearest Slime-Grubber, hurtling it backwards into the current. She fought her way down to reach Harold Foot-Webb. But seeing the wrench swing towards them, the others did not wait. They somersaulted backwards into the foam.

'You won't win,' yelled Sir Bounders Green. 'In a few minutes when the chamber is full, you'll all be drowned! I'm going off to tell the Princess you're dead, Ex-Prime Minister Foot-Webb. Then she'll have to marry *me*.'

With that, he and his gang dived straight into the middle of the swirling pool, down through a seething underwater outlet where the deluge was pumping in – and they were away.

As Suzie helped the creatures up to the top walkway, they heard, above the torrent, a harsh metallic ringing from the other side of the sluice.

Then all at once, like a huge bath emptying, the great soup of eels, mice, foam, the wretched drowned Rat, and the set of false teeth, drained itself in one torrential gulp.

Harold Foot-Webb was very nervous indeed when Suzie told him about the maintenance man.

'You must go back, or he'll come looking for you. We *cannot* be seen by a Human. We'll hide here and wait for you. Everything stops in Flood Conditions. No one can get around – except for those blasted Slime-Grubbers. It's almost dawn, and the moment the flood water goes down we must wade back to the Abbey to join our army.'

'May we come with you, Ex-Prime Minister?' requested the eight large Rats. 'After that nasty encounter with the Slime-Grubbers, we're on your side. We promise to protect you . . . and we know the way to the Abbey. Even after the storm water-level drops it will be difficult and slow to wade through the current.'

Harold Foot-Webb observed the Rats carefully. They did look very sorry for themselves. Also he needed to get to his army – fast. With the Queen's Slime-Grubber forces still about, they would help protect him.

'All right. But you do realize you'll now be under my command?'

'Where are you, girl?' the man called suddenly from the doorway. 'I told you to stay in my room.' The great shadowy figure leaned over the walkway. 'What are you doing down in the sewers anyway? I'm afraid I'll have to report this incident.' His head-torch flashed down the rungs. Harold Foot-Webb cringed and flung himself behind the Rats. But the torch light came to rest on Sir Pig Without Porkfolio, and it stayed there while the man's voice softened. 'Hold on! What have we here? Well now, little chappie, where exactly did *you* come from?'

Suzie pushed the Pig quickly up ahead, trying to keep the man's attention focused on it, and not the Sludge-Gulper. She talked all the time.

'I was trying to rescue the Pig. A manhole was left open. We both fell in . . . We nearly drowned. If it hadn't been for me alerting you just now, you might've drowned as well.' Quickly Suzie pushed the bewildered Pig in front and posted him through the door so that the man had to go in as well. 'Perhaps it's me who should be report-ing *you*? There was a radio on, far too loud to her anything else . . . like flooding.'

The man's voice immediately became serious.

'Maybe you're right. I was lucky. I would've been fired, for failing in my duty to check the sluice. But I can't understand how it came to be shut.'

By then Suzie was through the door, and closed it quickly behind her.

'I admit then, you more or less saved my bacon.' He grinned at the Pig, and bent to scratch at his back with hard, dirty finger-nails. 'And I expect she's just saved yours, too, little chappie. Whoops! Sorry! Didn't mean to offend.'

Suzie glared at him.

'I'll put the kettle on for tea. Come and dry yourselves.' He motioned them towards the fire. 'I'm Mr Barking, top "Security and Mainten-ance" around here. It's my job to make sure all required safety procedures are carefully adhered to. So thank you for alerting me to the danger.' And he held out an enormous hand that was rather hairy, and grasped Suzie's hand a little too hard. 'But it did look as if someone had wedged the flood-gate closed on purpose. It's all very fishy. No one's allowed down the sewers under any circumstances. I'll need to make a thorough investigation . . . and we'd better ring your parents – it's terribly late.'

'No . . . Please don't do that . . . My parents are asleep.'

'Asleep? They'll be half dead with worry!'

'But you don't understand,' said Suzie,

quickly. 'They're not at home. They're spending the night beside the Royal Route . . . in sleeping bags.'

'Oh, then they'll be sopping wet from the storm, like you. All right, I'll drive you to them after you've dried out. Then I must get back to work. The Abdication Ceremony starts at 10.15 a.m. and there's a set schedule of security arrangements to attend to throughout the night. There now, tea's up. Have a biscuit.'

It was lovely for Suzie to sit by the warm glow of the fire, clutching a hot mug of tea, and munching biscuits while water steamed off her clothes. She looked round the room; the walls were covered with maps and plans with black lines drawn all over them where the sewers went along under London. On the mantelpiece was a row of wine bottles, filled with specimens of river water, each dated and labelled. Suzie was encouraged to see that those with the most recent dates had less sediment than those from former years. Next to these was a large framed photograph of a dog, with 'Flusher' printed below.

While she drank, Suzie was trying to form a plan of escape. Absent-mindedly she worked her way through the whole packet of biscuits – giving one or two to the Pig.

'Tell me more about your job. What are those

181

special sewer torches you wear round your head?' she asked. 'They look really interesting.'

'Yes, they're very clever, these sewer lamps. They fit on to a band like a crown, and they can be adjusted to any head size. They light the way, and allow both hands to be free. These modern batteries are pretty good, too – they last for a whole year. Well now, I've a few calls to make. Then, when you're ready,' he said, taking the sewer lamp and hanging it back on the peg, 'I'll drive you down the route to your parents.'

'If you like,' said Suzie, yawning sleepily.

'. . . Admiralty Arch Security here. Barking speaking. Everything all right at the Hammersmith Depot? Any damage to report from the flash-flood?'

Suzie felt increasingly hot and tired. There was a hollow aching behind her eyes. Long before Mr Barking had got through all his checking, both she and the pig had fallen fast asleep.

Up above, Mrs Stanmore was making an anguished phone call to the police.

'My daughter, Suzie, is missing. Please help me find her. She's eleven, and she's got long floppy blond hair, blue eyes, a pale face, slim build . . .'

'Madam, we'll try, but youngsters are missing

all over London. We've had countless calls. I expect she's somewhere along the Royal Route, bagging her place with her friends. Everyone's sheltering from the pouring rain. We weren't expecting this storm – we're being worked off our feet coping with emergencies. But of course we'll put a call out straight away. Ring us if she comes back on her own.'

Storm water from as far as Highgate and Hampstead had charged downhill through the sewers below central London. Rainwater outlets spouted, Overflow Chambers overflowed, Tumbling Bays tumbled.

Queen Greenmould's army, which had been drilled and ready to advance, had scattered. Every Rat scampered from the flood to the safety of shelving over the High Interceptory Level Sewer, or waited in Expansion Chambers. Others crept into disused drains and outfall pipes which, being blocked, were nicely high and dry. All they could do was wait.

Under Covent Garden, the Sauna Baths were awash with rain. Operation Royal Flush, ready to set off, had had to abandon its advance. Forming a relay team, the Sludge-Gulper Army moved its Anti-Germ Warfare weapons up on to the disused platform at Covent Garden to keep them dry. There they huddled, waiting for the flood waters to subside. Rats loyal to the cause crouched next to fitfully slumbering Sludge-Gulpers along the whole length of the platform – like homeless 'bombed-out' refugees, sheltering from the Second World War.

In another of Bazalgette's sewers, Frogmorton, Rickmansworthy and Purley got away from the flood by squeezing themselves inside a large rain-water gully. There they waited in an agony of impatience for the water swirling around them to go down. They had reached the depth of despair: no leaders, no prop, and hardly any time left.

'The Alligator must've eaten Suzie, the Pig Without Porkfolio, and Ex-Prime Minister Foot-Webb. A most terrible, terrible death,' said Rickmansworthy, his voice reduced to a broken croak.

'But they would want us to carry on,' insisted Purley. 'As soon as the flood subsides, we'd better wade back to the Sauna Baths. Our army couldn't have set out – or got very far – with this flood. Let's see if it's dried out and join it.'

'We'll have to lead them now,' said Frogmorton. 'If Operation Royal Flush fails to straighten the prop, it will be the end of us all.'

*

Behind Mr Barking's security door, at the bottom of the Expansion Chamber, eight shaggy Rats peered at one another and narrowed their eyes at Ex-Prime Minister Foot-Webb. The same evil thought struck them all. They overcame the Sludge-Gulper easily, and held his arms firmly behind his back. Then they dragged him struggling from the chamber and stuffed him into an outflow pipe, a little too small for him. There they waited, holding him prisoner throughout the night. When the flood waters went down, they would frogmarch him to the Queen and claim their reward.

Underneath Westminster Abbey, the Company of Grey Rats had taken over Parliament Under Parliament for the duration of the flood. They filled the House of Lords which, set higher up, remained untouched from the danger. There they discussed how they would put into effect the careful plan they had nursed through their debate in the Think-Tank. When the water level lowered they would be ready to act.

Everything in the London sewers had been brought to a halt during the storm.

Only the Slime-Grubbers had been abroad,

riding the foam and swimming effortlessly through the swiftly running current. Having left the Queen's enemies to drown, they went on to capture anything hurtling by that could be used to build a mighty contraption for the Pulling Team, so they could whisk away the throne and Royal Regalia. Already they had found a car tyre, polythene sheeting, a child's scooter, and the chassis of a pram. Two skateboards had been discovered trapped against a weir sluice. The main part of the Contraption, needed to catch the throne, had been skilfully formed from four plastic milk-crates and two supermarket trolleys – one from Sainsbury's, the other from Tesco. To soften Her Majesty's fall, mail-bags from under Mount Pleasant Sorting Office had been strung all around, tied into position with labels stating, 'T. Wells', 'Snodland' and 'Sevenoaks, Kent'.

In a nice dry Expansion Chamber under the Whitechapel Road, a group of female Slime-Grubbers had cleverly twirled together a harness for the team of Rats, who were to pull the Contraption. It was made from frayed nylon rope, old rag, hair from plugholes, and thread from below the clothing factories. Her Majesty would be delighted.

CHAPTER TWENTY

The Storm Channels

J ust before daybreak, the Storm Channels in the sewers had dealt with the extra flow of rainwater, pumping gallons of it over the weirs until most of the deluge had been dealt with and drained away. Soon the flood-level had dropped enough for creatures other than Slime-Grubbers to get around.

Before the first morning tube train went by, the Sludge-Gulpers and Rats began ferrying their ammunition down from the disused platform at Covent Garden to the Sauna Baths below. That was when Frogmorton, Rickmansworthy and Purley arrived, sopping wet, having forced their way through strong currents to get back and give their appalling news.

'Then it's Action Stations,' ordered Edna, gravely. 'Troops, are you ready to march? There are only a few hours to go.'

Outside the Palace gates, Queen Greenmould was in a filthy mood.

'Pompey! Pompey, where *are* you?' she called. 'Why hasn't my Alligator returned?'

'Oh your Majesty!' cried Lady Loo, who accompanied her. 'Not only are we now without Pompey, but he's probably eaten your Hand-Maiden, who was going to dangle beneath the throne.'

'Yes, you're right, Lady Loo,' the Queen snapped. 'But one cannot be faultless always. I admit that was a foolish move. One got carried away – overcoming the opposition by having it eaten. When Pompey comes back, perhaps we could leave him below the throne at the very last minute. Pompey! Pompey!'

'Ratty-Ratty-Ratty-Rats!' called Lady Loo, temptingly.

'Don't shout like that, oaf! Do you want the Rats to hear?'

'They won't. All the Rats are still in hiding from the storm. Pompey will be back. He wouldn't dream of missing his morning Rats, would he?'

'One is not so sure. He may not need any breakfast, having devoured that One-Off . . . as well as Prime Minister Foot-Webb.'

'He'll've eaten our Wedding feast, too – roast pork, remember?'

'Yes.' Queen Greenmould looked sulky. 'You needn't rub it in, Lady Loo. King Gropius will be raving mad about that – we'd better not tell him. I suppose one had better be grateful for shepherd's pie, instead. Oh dear, with *her* gone, I suppose it'll be one's final pie.'

But her mood brightened considerably when, with a tremendous rattling, the finished Contraption drew up. Eagerly, its proud makers – Sir Bounders Green and his gang of Slime-Grubbers – slithered from their masterpiece to the ground and stood in line to attention.

The Queen pressed her clammy hands together, and began immediately to issue orders.

'Right! Now for a Pulling Team. Have you organized it, Lady Loo?'

'I trained some Rats . . . but then they escaped to shelter from the flood.'

'Start winkling them out . . . Find some more . . . large ones. You, Slime-Grubbers, one is sending you as a contingent of guards to see that no one gets near the trap for the Abdication Ceremony. As for my newly titled Grubbers, you must re-assemble my army, *fast*. Get it searched out, dried out and re-drilled. Even if a Sludge-Gulper army *has* been formed under those steam baths, it won't have been able to set out during the flood – but it will before long. Our outfit will be called "Operation Steamroller". It must

189

be ready to advance after breakfast. Only then, Sir Bounders Green, can you come to claim Princess Griselda for your bride.'

The tired-looking Slime-Grubbers were dismissed.

Queen Greenmould's next plan was to requisition Igor, her daughter's pet Rat, to head the Pulling Team. He was the strongest Rat around. She made straight for Princess Griselda's room to fetch him. Bursting in, she found to her surprise, the Belisha beacons flashing on and off in an empty room.

'Funny! . . . One smells a Rat,' she cried. 'Or rather, one doesn't! Where's Igor?' she screamed. 'He's needed. Where's Princess Griselda? She should be here. She's getting married today.'

She was answered by a familiar gurgling sound. 'Quick! One cannot afford to miss one's Royal morning bath. Her Majesty is up and bathing early on her final day – there's bound to be something really smelly.'

Princess Griselda had been up at the crack of dawn. Taking her pet Rat with her, she waded secretly to the French Embassy, watching out for danger on the way. While taking a wedding bath, the Princess poured out her feelings of despair to Igor.

'Where, where is Squidgy? He promised to come and claim me,' she sobbed. 'The Abdication Ceremony is scheduled for 10.15; my wedding is to be at 11.00. If he doesn't come I'll be forced to marry that scaly Bounders Green. Don't leave me, Igor. Help me, please.'

'I will stay with you and protect you, I promise. We will act normally in front of the Queen so that she doesn't suspect us. If Harold arrives with the army, we will let it into the Palace, as arranged. But if nobody comes at all, then you must be ready to desert with me to the East End.'

Satisfied with their scheme, they took advantage of the first two baths, before going back. The Princess was swamped in 'Pour l'Homme', while Igor reeked of 'Evening in Paris'.

But when she returned to the Palace, Princess Griselda found, to her utter horror, that she was still too fat to fit into her wedding gown.

'When Harold comes to claim me, I won't be ready. Oh, where *is* he?'

At that moment, Harold Foot-Webb was being brutally hauled along by the eight large, shaggy Rats. They had almost reached the Palace. Once the flood waters had decreased sufficiently they had started out straight away, eager to claim the five hundred button reward. The Sludge-Gulper despaired. He might just as well be dead, the

Queen would kill him anyway once they arrived. He let his body go lifeless . . . so that he was exceptionally difficult to drag along.

In the Maintenance and Security Office, Suzie awoke with a start. Mr Barking had returned from making his rounds.

'I let you stay asleep because you were exhausted and still wet,' he said, considerately. 'I didn't want you to catch pneumonia.'

'How long have I been asleep?' Suzie panicked.

'Only a few hours, while I was doing security checks. Now that dawn has broken and the storm is over, I'll drive you back to your parents. Don't bother waking the pig, I'll look after him.'

Suzie shot a look of terror towards the Swamp Pig – she couldn't leave him with this horrid man. She would have to think of something fast. Nor could they begin searching for parents she'd invented. She couldn't just wake up any old parents down the Royal Route and say, 'Hello, Mum and Dad!'

Mr Barking had almost reached the door that led up a flight of stairs to the street. Suzie was desperate. What could she do?

'I'll drive the van round to the door as it's wet. Be ready to jump in.'

This was her chance. Immediately Mr Barking left, Suzie woke the Pig and told him they had to leave sharpish. She grabbed a sewer torch from its peg and rammed it on to her head. Then she decided on a waterproof jacket that was so large it was like a mac. She stole some string from the table to tighten it round her waist, quickly rolled up the sleeves, and opened the door to the sewer . . . Then she had a good idea. She streaked to the street door, which the maintenance man had left ajar, and flung it wide open. 'He'll think we've left that way – he won't even bother to check down the sewer.'

Suzie switched on her splendid new sewer lamp. Immediately a strong circle of light sprang from her brow, leaving both hands free to climb down the rungs and support the Pig. But the Inspection Chamber was empty: no Harold Foot-Webb, no eight large Rats. They looked down the Sewer entrances. Nothing!

'They would've hurried back to the Abbey to help the army pull up the prop,' the Pig reasoned. 'Let's join them.'

'But we don't know where we are, do we?'

'Didn't you hear Mr Barking say that this was Admiralty Arch on the phone?' the Pig said, proudly. 'I did, and I know exactly where we are – it's no distance at all. We go down the

Whitehall Sewer, then into Embankment Sewer, and we're practically there. Come on!'

The atmosphere was slimy and damp. Water evaporated in steamy clouds, eerily lit by Suzie's head-lamp. The flood water dripped from overhead, making it feel as if it was raining underground. Suzie was pleased with her new mac. It preserved some of the warmth she'd gained from Mr Barking's electric fire, and acted like a tea-cosy to keep her warm. One or two creatures, slinking from their hiding places, blinked blindly in the glare of her sewer light, then shook themselves dry and began to groom their fur. But Suzie and the Swamp Pig raced along effortlessly, because the strong current was going their way.

CHAPTER TWENTY-ONE

The Grey Rats

Morning had broken on Abdication Day. Streams of multicoloured light poured through the stained glass windows in Westminster Abbey. Shooting through pitch-black shadows, they wandered in patterns across the carpet or collected in countless pools on the polished floor. Beautifully arranged flowers emerged from the shadows to display themselves from every shelf. Fingers of light felt across a marble Knight with his Lady lying at his side, so that they seemed to shift slightly in their sleep and almost to wake. Silver candlesticks sparkled, and the great gold cross glinted on the altar. The dark shape, soon picked out as Edward I's highly polished ancient wooden throne, gleamed regally . . . but leaned at least half an inch to the right.

Big Ben chimed six. There was a deep *crash*!

The Abbey door opened, lights were switched on, people poured in and security guards with walkie-talkies checked the place over. Vergers put service leaflets on to pews. A camera crew arrived to test the lighting and sound for television. Spotlights were switched on and directed towards the throne.

'*One . . . Two . . . Three . . . Four . . . Testing.*'

Suzie and the Pig heard the ghostly chimes of Big Ben strike six as they raced through the Ratacombs towards the prop. But when they reached it, a much greater shock awaited them. Flickering beams, a thousand times more startling than Suzie's lamp, glowed in a golden light. It looked as if the tunnel was on fire. Suzie froze, switched off her sewer lamp, and stepped back into the shadows, shielding the Pig behind her.

There, waiting silently, was what looked like the entire Ancient Order of Grey Rats. Each Sacred Rat held aloft a long taper, which had been lit one after another from the Houses of Parliament central heating boiler. The sight was extraordinarily magical – yet almost alarming. And they need not have bothered to hide, for the Grey Rats had either seen – or sensed – their presence.

'I will not be afraid,' said Suzie, quietly, as

the two of them somehow became intricately involved in the procession, drawn along, woven carefully among the Rats, on and on up the tunnel, wound round tight, as if trapped in the centre of a soft ball of wool. Then one of them spoke.

'I am Ignatius, Head of the Sacred Rats. Do not be afraid. We are here to protect you. My Sect has been observing you closely. We know the Pig is now on your side. Greenmould's plan to steal the crown and throne can only lead to the end of us all. We will help, but we may not fight – it is not permitted. Disaster approaches fast – there is barely time. Follow me.'

Suzie and the Swamp Pig found themselves marshalled along to where the Acro-prop still leaned over, crooked and useless, lit by a circle of flaming tapers stuck into the mud. Beside it was the net, neatly folded, and Pompey's chain, coiled like a snake, with the Union Jack flag folded on top.

Suzie gasped. Why wasn't their army here to right it? Where was Harold Foot-Webb? Purley? Frogmorton? Rickmansworthy? Her heart quickened, her mouth dried out. She walked wretchedly around wondering what to do. In that damaged state the prop could not *possibly* support the Queen. And all the while, not far from the Abbey, Big Ben was ticking the seconds away.

What were her plans if no one came at all? Somehow try to escape? Maybe go through the cloister manhole with the Pig up into the Abbey? But how could they pretend they'd been invited? Imagine what the people in their beautiful clothes would think, seeing one of the guests wearing an odd, outsize mac, accompanied by a small, smelly pig? And if she warned them about the throne, how could she explain the trap? They would interrogate her mercilessly, but would never believe her story . . .

'What shall we do, Suzie?' squealed the Pig. 'The Queen will sit on her throne in a few hours' time.'

As if to rub in this fact, Big Ben reminded them it was half past six.

'We'll need a huge source of strength if we're to pull up the prop – like an army. Wait! Listen! Here it comes!' Suzie rejoiced at the sound of noisy splashing echoing up the tunnel. At last Operation Royal Flush had arrived!

Then her blood turned to ice. A scratching and shrill jabbering accompanied the row, as a contingent of Slime-Grubber guards came into view, sent by Queen Greenmould to protect the leaning prop and re-adjust the fishing net beneath.

The Slime-Grubbers had not been expecting these strange Grey Rats. But they were slight, rather small – easy to fight. Yes, look! They were already parting on either side of the tunnel into two great lines, forming a processional arch under which the Slime-Grubber victors would be allowed to pass. The scaly creatures marched through, blinking in the glaring lights. There was something most unsettling about this silent vigil and the reproachful looks fixed upon them. They hesitated to attack. At first they were amazed, then nervous, finally afraid, as they slunk along, dragging their feet . . . slower and slower. They were unable to deal with the Grey Rats separating like a great zip-fastener in front, then closing in behind, fastening the zip shut.

The Slime-Grubbers shook fearfully, their jabbering ceased, the scales on their backs slackened. Soon they were hypnotized to a halt, unable to go any further.

No violence was used as the Sacred Rats pressed in with their wide, penetrating eyes. They came so close with their flaming tapers that they almost singed the Slime-Grubbers' scales. Their victims waited powerless, tails between legs, while they were surrounded. Then the Grey Rats fanned out and, holding a piece of the net each, flung it over the stupefied guards as if they were catching a shoal of fish. The net was then dragged along to be re-hung under the throne.

Suzie was delighted with the Grey Rats' victory. She sat on the Union Jack folded over the coil of chain, and watched the captive Greenbacks writhe and struggle in their cocoon. But still her army did not arrive, and soon she was back to feelings of despair. Her hand clutched at the mound she was sitting on, then she got up and looked at it. Pompey's chain was very long, and the Grey Rats were terribly skimpy . . . but maybe, just maybe . . . if a dozen or so pulled one behind the other, they might be able to ease the prop upright again. They could *try*.

Suzie took off her heavy mac and put it safely in the dry with the Union Jack, then looped the chain round the Acro. Bravely she began to command:

'Some of you Grey Rats, get behind me. Pull when I say. Ignatius, grab the end of the chain. Don't let go – dig your paws hard into the ground. One, two, three, *pull*! Again . . . *One, two, three, pullll*!'

It was useless. The prop wouldn't budge.

Suzie undid the extra length of chain they had used to brace the prop. She joined this to the end of the Alligator's chain. Then she got every single Grey Rat in the Sect to heave, putting Sir

Pig Without Porkfolio on the end so that his hoofs could dig into the mud.

'*One, two, three, pull*!' she cried. '*One, two, three, pullll*!'

The prop shifted ever so slightly . . . but not nearly enough to yank it into place.

Just then Big Ben chimed seven, shivering down from what felt like directly overhead.

'Oh dear!' she cried. 'What we need is one colossal weight to give a massive jolt. Pig, what shall we do?' She turned to the Pig . . . but he was no longer holding the chain. He had disappeared.

Up Above, the organist, having warmed up, was now well into his stride, practising the anthem. Thunderous chords reverberated through the Abbey. The choir chatted excitedly, emitting a few nervous top warbles and one or two scales to loosen their throats, while they went into the Vestry to sort out their vestments. The bell-ringers began to arrive.

Suzie was at her wit's end. Why had the Pig deserted her now, just when she needed him most? Had he escaped so that he wouldn't be blamed when the Queen tumbled through?

Many of the Grey Rats, too, seemed to have melted away. Where *was* her army?

Operation Royal Flush, armed with plentiful supplies of Anti-Germ Warfare, set off bravely from the Sauna Baths and marched steadily towards Trafalgar Square. Purley, Frogmorton and Rickmansworthy were joint commanders. Behind them, in the front line, Edna Pongworthy, Angel Rat, Steaming Lil and Jacusi kept up a marching song in high-pitched raucous voices:

> 'Gulpers croak and Rats must screech,
> Get the blighters with our bleach!'

At the rear, their Rats were led by Chigwell, Shadwell and Angel. Only Grandad and Granny Gulper had stayed behind, to look after Flotsam, Jetsam and all the Gulper children.

The big High Interceptory Level was the widest and most sensible route for an army to take, before turning south down Whitehall Sewer to Westminster. Big Ben had just struck quarter to eight, and there was no time for delay. They were well aware that the Queen would have her booby trap heavily guarded. They'd have to fight their way through to prop it up before the Queen Up Above sat down on her throne. After the Abdication Ceremony was over, they intended to storm the Sewer Palace and avenge the deaths of their leaders who had surely been eaten by Pompey. Queen Greenmould herself would be killed.

CHAPTER TWENTY-TWO

Princess Griselda

Big Ben struck eight on Abdication Day. A fiery hot sun rose up to evaporate the rain that drenched the tarmac along the Royal Route. It was a brilliant beginning. Flowers opened, flags unfurled, foreign diplomats arrived. Subjects sleeping on the pavements to get the best positions waited for the rainbow before hanging wet sleeping bags over the railings to dry.

Inside the Palace, attendants laid out costumes, ladies-in-waiting rushed about. Down in the kitchens, the Royal corgis ran to and fro getting under everybody's feet.

'Get these animals out of the way,' shouted a Footman, 'before they send someone flying.'

In the Palace courtyard, the great golden coach was enjoying its final polish, and beyond the gates, people poured from tube stations to occupy any remaining spaces down the Mall. On

Abdication Day, travelling on the underground was free.

In the weak watery rays that filtered from around a manhole cover at the end of the Mall, Lady Loo returned from catching some very large Rats by their tails, forcing them to join her team for the Pulling Contraption. As she passed beneath the fountain outside Buckingham Palace, she looked to see if Pompey had returned to have his morning drink. He hadn't – but along the tunnel a strange bedraggled figure appeared, hauled with great difficulty through the sludge by eight exultant Rats.

'Where's the Queen? We've come to claim our five hundred button reward.'

Lady Loo peered closely at the figure, then chuckled.

'Why, if it isn't Ex-Prime Minister Foot-Webb! I thought you'd expired!'

He was hardly recognizable, so mud-covered was he, so humiliated and drained of life. She would prolong this elegant torture a little longer.

'Rats, her Majesty will be underneath Westminster Abbey, ready with her reward for you, at exactly 10.15. Be there!'

As the wretched Sludge-Gulper was dragged

away once more, Lady Loo clutched her webbed hands together. Those Rats would be perfect for helping to pull the Royal throne away – she would add them to her team at the very last minute. And how she would *enjoy* Harold Foot-Webb's humiliation as he watched the tumbling take place. 'As he's in safe hands, I won't need to inform anyone that he's still alive – just yet,' she resolved, as she went in for breakfast. 'Griselda must marry Sir Bounders Green instead. He should be here to claim her.'

Looking very keen and eager, Sir Bounders Green had already squirmed his way along to the Palace, and burst into the Throne Room far too early. On his way to claim his bride, he had bumped into Lady Foulness, waiting to go in for breakfast. Sir Bounders Green had been able to inform her, very smugly, that his rival, Harold Foot-Webb, was drowned: 'Don't tell Grisely for the time being, Foulness. She might cry, and there has been quite enough water around here already.'

He greeted his fiancée: 'Hello, Precious Lump.' His scales were shiny and wet, his tail polished and horribly green.

The Princess was sitting on her Throne Root quietly crying. Her true fiancé had still not arrived. She scowled at her first fiancé as he bowed so low that his wrinkled snout almost scraped the sludge. The thought of being married to this foul creature and living in the Palace with him for ever, made hard steel pipes ring round her heart and squeeze in until she could barely breathe. At her feet, Igor growled.

'Bouncing Beauty,' said Sir Bounders Green, 'the booby trap is laid, the Pulling Contraption made. My army is re-assembled and waiting ready at your command – and so am I.'

'Where's my wedding gift?' queried Princess Griselda.

Her first fiancé quenched his smile.

'Have you got my engagement ring yet?'

Her fiancé looked guilty.

'Have you even found me a wedding ring?'

Her fiancé hung his head.

'If you've not got a single thing to give me, how can I marry you? I shall wait for my true fiancé to arrive.'

'Anything, I'll get anything you want, Fat Love,' he offered. 'What is it you require?'

Bending to pat her Rat, a strange look passed over the Princess's face. Then looking up with a beaming smile, she answered, touchingly:

'A Royal corgi.'

*

Sir Bounders Green made for the Palace Up Above. Now that he had successfully drowned his rival, he felt obliged not to disappoint his bride. Anyway, all this hard work had almost reached fruition. Soon, his real scheme could begin. He aimed to kill King Gropius – by adding more and more Rat poison to his drink. Later he would dispatch Queen Greenmould – by some equally ghastly method. Then *he*, having married the Princess, would inherit everything, enjoying the Throne and Crown for himself. Queen Griselda would have to be content to be 'Consort with Corgi', on the ordinary Root by his side . . . 'And the corgi will displace and chase away that stupid pet Rat,' he muttered as he stealthily crept up the huge pipe that drained the whole of the Buckingham Palace Courtyard.

Loosening the grating with his snout, he crawled silently out and crept along, hugging the shadows close to the gutter. Then he scaled the Palace walls like a lizard, and made for a large window. The Queen's drawing-room window had been opened a little to let the sun stream in. Sir Bounders Green eased himself through. From there he made a terrific *leap* down on to the carpet, right into the middle of the Queen's Royal corgis.

The corgis were in a terrible mood. They had been shut in because they had been in everyone's way ... *and they still had not been fed*. Seeing this nice green scaly thing wriggling in their midst, they stopped barking immediately. He was as large as themselves and twice as long – easily enough for all. Greedily they ate the Slime-Grubber for breakfast. He was an interesting flavour.

Queen Greenmould, still smelling furiously from her heavily scented bath, made quickly for the dining room and looked up expectantly for breakfast. Lady Loo joined her, exhausted from rounding up Rats. 'Where's one's husband, Lady Loo?' enquired the Queen, crossly.

'Please Ma'am, King Gropius went out boozing last night, and hasn't returned.'

'Where's Sir Bounders Green? He's meant to present one with one's army and claim his bride. He's late.'

'Don't know, Ma'am. He should have arrived by now.'

'Where's Pompey? Was he waiting back here for breakfast?'

'Please Ma'am, no Ma'am.'

'Where's Griselda and her Rat? They've some explaining to do. It's the man who normally goes out for a Stag-Beetle party the night before marrying – not the bride and her Rat,' she remarked, scathingly. 'One is becoming pretty livid on such an important day.'

Just then, Lady Foulness arrived for breakfast.

'Please Ma'am, the Princess *is* back. She's sitting in the Throne Room with Igor. She's asked to be excused breakfast so she can fit into her dress. She says she's waiting for her true fiancé to arrive.'

'That's because she doesn't know yet that he's an *Ex*-Ex-Prime Minister – ha ha ha – because he was eaten by Pompey at my command. Don't tell her, though, or even when the wedding gown does fit, it'll be too sopping wet when Sir Bounders Green comes to claim her.'

Lady Foulness frowned, rather puzzled. She'd been told that the second fiancé had been drowned, not eaten . . . The first fiancé had told her just a while back . . . and hadn't he already been to claim his bride?

'Ah! Here's breakfast! Quick!' The Queen reached out for her corgi bowl. 'Soon, Lady Loo, it will be time to send my army off. After that, it will be time to harness the Pulling Team.'

King Gropius also missed the final breakfast of shepherd's pie. It was almost half past eight before he appeared, and he could barely stand.

''Cos Daddy wouldn't buy you a bow-wow-

wow,' he sang in falsetto to Griselda and Igor.
'Mmmm, what a foul mixture of Pour l'Homme
and Evening in Paris. Terrific!'

The Queen rushed in to be on her Root in
time. She was so full that she could hardly make
it. She had eaten her helping, the Princess's helping, King Gropius' helping, and also that of Sir
Bounders Green. But when she saw the King
lurching, she was beside herself with rage.

'*Gropius*! I've *never* seen you so drunk! You'll
be in no fit state for your daughter's wedding!
You do realize it's to take place at eleven?'

'Couldn't get you a Royal corgi, Grisely dear.
Did try. Saw all this marvellous Abdication
Champagne though, on the way, in Buckingham
Palace cellars. "Luvelly, luvelly, bubbley stuff",'
he sang. 'Drank bottles of the stuff. Brought
back tons. Loads more where they came from.
They won't miss it. Hiccup! Brought you these
instead, Grisely dear, but as they're blue, I suppose I'd better give them to your mother. Here,
m'dear. Mmmm, you smell nice, too. "Lily of
the Alley" was it?'

'Ooh! What are these?' The Queen's anger
subsided slightly as she picked up the pretty blue
tubes.

'They're from the firework display over the
Serpentine tonight. Won't miss 'em. Thousands
more. Let's start the day off with a bang.'

He lit one for her with his methane gas lighter. It whizzed straight for the Coat of Arms and burnt a hole through the Bar Sinister, bounced off the wall and skeetered from one side of the sewer to the other, then, still fizzling, drowned itself in the fountain. The Queen frowned.

'I hope that is not a bad omen, Gropey! Nothing must go wrong today – it is *vital* for my plot to succeed. Drainpipes and filth will be moved to make sure it does. Even though one has no Pig, no Hand-Maiden, the Alligator's gone, the Bridegroom's disappeared, my army's still not ready . . . That leaves just you, Igor, and you must be ready to head one's Pulling Team in under one hour's time.'

'What do you mean, *no Pig*!' King Gropius exclaimed.

'You can't have Igor, he's mine!' screamed Griselda. 'If you chain him to your Contraption he'll get killed by the police when they investigate your plot. Igor's going to be my page and hold up my train.'

Igor looked magnificent. His velvety ears were brushed, his coat sleek and shiny, his white muzzle washed, his long whiskers profusely waxed. Round his neck he wore a big bow tie in royal colours of red, white and blue.

'What about roast pork? That's what I want to know!' the King howled, almost apoplectic.

'There's no need to worry about that Alligator, Mouldy – Pompey's bound to be back for his next meal, hiccup! He wouldn't get through a single day without his *Rats* to eat, would he?'

At Grisely's feet, the ropy tail of Igor stiffened round her ankle. His eyes narrowed, his fur bristled, causing the bow tie to rise like a ruff about his neck.

'You *idiot*, Gropius! That's a Court Secret! It's just like you to muck things up at this stage!' The Queen flushed crimson, as the blue ink distilled from her blood and drained to her feet. She stood and threatened her husband with the sceptre. 'Soggy old cesspit! Can't you stop boozing for a single second?'

Gropius staggered towards the Rat.

'Sorry . . . stupid mistake, Igor, old chap. Didn't really mean it. Nasty joke to tease you, eh what? Here, have a cigar.'

But Igor had reared up hissing, and with claws outstretched, sprang at the King.

'Ooaaggh!' cried Griselda, as the knot tightened round her ankle, and toppled her into the mud.

Igor snarled. He undid his tail with his teeth. He wrenched the bow tie off with his claws and trampled it in the mud. Next, he leapt on to the Root and crouched there as if ready to spring. His muscles rippled, red eyes darted from King

213

to Queen, and his hackles were up, making him look tremendous.

'The moment has finally *come*!' he screeched, thwacking his tail hard against the Root. 'Although I fell victim to the life of shepherd's pie, from now on everything will change. I've realized what's been going on and I'm ready to fight. I'll lead every Sewer Rat against you, Greenmould, and we'll overthrow the Throne.'

With that, he shot off the Root and bolted.

The Queen stood, silent and swaying, while her blotched face flashed from one colour to the next, like traffic lights gone berserk. Then her sceptre suddenly swirled around her head, as she yelled, 'After him, Pompey. Get him!'

But Pompey wasn't there.

'Lady Loo, then, will help me form a Rattery – huge creatures with great biting power – Killer Rats they'll be, you'll see. Lady Loo, go and harness the team to one's Contraption immediately! We must be ready to depart at half past nine! Gather round, everybody else. You're to pay attention to one's orders.'

She turned to face an empty Court. The ladies-in-waiting had fled. King Gropius lay in a heap on the floor, having passed out after Igor's attack, like cold water down the plughole.

Princess Griselda was thinking hard. Her Rat had deserted her – when he had promised to guard her. He had elected to fight with the Rats. She would have to cope with her mad mother completely alone. She got up off the mud and brushed herself down. Then, summoning all her courage, she sat up very straight on her Root. This was the moment when she would have to show her true feelings. After this, she would no longer be able to pretend. This was the turning-point of her whole life.

The Queen had turned to her daughter.

'Forget about your Rat, Griselda. It's your future husband one's worried about now. If Sir Bounders Green doesn't turn up soon with the army ready to go, you will have to marry Lord Kenzal Green.'

'*Never*!' shrieked Griselda, jumping up in fury.

'Then it shall be the Honourable Harry Neasden – you shouldn't be so fussy. Where's Sir Bounders Green got to, that's what I'd like to know?'

'I sent him Up Above. To fetch a Royal corgi for my wedding gift.'

'*What?* You stupid, ungrateful child! He'll *never* return – that's *far* too dangerous a thing to ask!'

'I already knew that,' answered Princess Griselda, softly.

'Silly girl to get rid of a fiancé like that!' said the Queen, uneasily. 'But one's having no nonsense. You *shall* marry Harry Neasden, or Lord Kenzal Green . . . or even the Duke of Dalston, if you prefer – they're all equally Upstream. Decide now, and I'll make the fiancé of your choice into a colonel to lead the army.'

Griselda gulped at her mother. Her large eyes narrowed to a slit, her yellow spots quivered and joined in a passion of pink. Her voice rose to a terrific pitch, cracking some mud from the ceiling.

'*No! No! No! I won't! Won't! Won't! I hate you, Mother – and I'm not afraid of you any more!*' Her voice was trembling with emotion. 'You have never cared for me or *my* happiness, Mother! You only wanted everything for yourself. You are wicked and treacherous. And because no one else has dared tell you, I would like to inform you that you are completely and utterly . . . *mad*!'

Princess Griselda had waited for this moment a long time. Resigning her Throne Root, she bounced towards the door. Her final words to her mother were filled with confidence and strength.

'No matter what *you* say, Mother . . . I'm leaving to live in the East End. And I *will* marry Harold Foot-Webb, so there!'

The Queen hurled a handful of sludge at her daughter.

'You can't. He's dead! Pompey ate him.'

Griselda stopped short at the door and turned to stare at her mother.

'My true fiancé . . . *Dead*?'

An unearthly shriek welled up from inside her. A wail of complete despair. '*Squidgy*!'

She rushed from the Palace distraught and almost out of her mind.

At that moment, Lady Loo hurtled back into the Throne Room, her face dark as ditchwater, her hands quivering in agitation above her head.

'Your Majesty! Your Majesty! The enemy is marching! They are heading along the High Interceptory Sewer towards Trafalgar Square. They must be coming to storm the Palace!'

The colour drained in one gulp from the Queen's hard face.

'Call Sir Kenzal Green! Call the Duke of Dalston! Call the Honourable Neasden!' she let rip. 'Our army must be ready to advance. *Now*!'

CHAPTER TWENTY-THREE

Igor the Rat

Queen Greenmould shot from the Palace Gates, wielding her sceptre. A short way in front of her, at the head of the Mall, she found Operation Steamroller waiting ready, impatient to be off. It was a colossal affair – threatening, full of confidence and power – composed as it was of practically every Slime-Grubber in the London Sewers, together with a great horde of Rats.

'Your Commander, Sir Bounders Green, is indisposed,' Queen Greenmould bellowed. 'The Honourable Harry Neasden will lead. The Duke of Dalston and Lord Kenzal Green are to bring up the rear. The Rattery shall be headed by Sir Tottenham Court Rat and the Honourable Oval Rat. March at ramming speed along the High Interceptory Sewer towards Trafalgar Square. There you will overcome the enemy – then go on to storm the Sauna Baths and destroy every creature without question. *Advance*!' yelled the Queen.

Operation Steamroller swarmed off in a great crawling mass of green scales and bristling fur.

Operation Royal Flush had reached Trafalgar Square, and was about to turn south into the Whitehall sewer, when it heard the churning of feet thundering along the High Interceptory Sewer from the direction of the Palace. Every fighter knew, without a word being exchanged, that it *had* to be the Queen's army, charging towards them. Although still far away, so immense was the terrible racket that it must have been made by a force several times the size of their own. They'd simply be trampled to death.

'Stop!' shouted Frogmorton. 'Let's stay here, stand firm and defend Trafalgar Square. Whatever happens, the Queen's army mustn't get past us to storm the Sauna Baths, or all our children will be killed.'

'And I say, let's get the blighters with our bleach!' yelled Steaming Lil.

'Yes,' cheered Jacusi. 'We're no yellow-bellies. We've got all our weapons. Let's show we're not afraid – let's face 'em head on!'

Their spontaneous courage was infectious.

219

Operation Royal Flush chorused its agreement and surged forward as fast as it could, to challenge the enemy, with Anti-Germ Warfare weapons poised at the ready.

As Big Ben struck half past nine, Queen Green-mould streaked back from sending off her army, having braced her spirits first by drinking mass-ive amounts of blue bubbles that leaked from below the Buckingham Palace fountain. Lady Loo was waiting ready for her mistress outside the Sewer Palace, holding in check her crack team of Rats. Baroness Squeaker-Brent and Viscount Wapping had been chosen to head the Pulling Contraption. Harnessed and ready to go, they were champing at the bit. Quickly mount-ing her Sainsbury's shopping trolley, the Queen gave the order to set out. Lady Foulness and the other ladies-in-waiting waved them off with their royal monogrammed hankies. Lady Loo, wedged in state beside her mistress in the basket from Tesco, cracked a whip of tied-together shoelaces to encourage the Team to slide through the sludge. Along the sewer they charged, choos-ing to travel under Victoria to Westminster, so as not to run into the back of their own army.

Up Above . . . also exactly as Big Ben struck

half past nine, Her Majesty the Queen, resplendent in heavy royal regalia and feeling a mixture of excitement and sadness, was helped into her shiny golden coach for her last official journey. It was a grand, historic occasion. A colossal crowd watched this final, splendid show. Slowly the coach wheeled through the Palace courtyard, then, escorted by the Household Cavalry, left Buckingham Palace amid a cheering crowd. It swept past the fountain and rolled along the Mall, under Admiralty Arch, around Trafalgar Square, then down Whitehall, gathering speed towards the Abbey. It was followed by other members of the Royal Family together with a vast procession of marching soldiers and massed regimental bands.

Beneath the Mall, Operation Royal Flush clashed headlong with Operation Steamroller. So powerful were the fumes, that the Queen's front line was hit even before it came into view. Slime-Grubbers gasped and fell back, or scrabbled from harm's way by swarming up the sodden sewer walls, to clutch and tear at the brickwork overhead. Enemy Rats turned tail, draining into any outlet they could find, even scampering over one another in their efforts to save their skins.

'We're being cleansed! We're being flushed out!' they howled in anguish.

To the enemy, every fighter wearing a bright J-Cloth over its nose seemed to be a member of some ghastly new species of Sewer Creature. The next front line cowered – still more attempted to flee. As their leading ranks crumpled, other Rats and Slime-Grubbers pushed in from behind in a relentless stream. But Operation Royal Flush's chemical warfare was most effective. They were gaining the upper hand. They began to push the Queen's army backwards along the Mall.

Queen Greenmould had reached Westminster. Her Contraption was just turning into the Ratacombs, when Baroness Squeaker-Brent reared up, shying in her traces, terrified by the guttering tapers of the Grey Rats that lined both sides of the tunnel to meet them. Next to her, Viscount Wapping did the same, causing the great Contraption to jolt to a halt.

'Out of my way!' screeched Queen Greenmould, cracking her whip towards the double row of eyes. Then she saw that they belonged to the Sacred Company of Grey Rats . . . and they seemed to be staring her out. Their tapers flamed and flickered in her face. It was uncanny and horrible, and had to be stopped.

'What is the meaning of this? Out of my way, little runts!' She cracked her whip so hard that it curled in the air and slashed through the neck of one of the sacred sect. There was scarcely a whimper as the small creature folded up and fell forward, lying lifeless on the tunnel floor.

Now the avenue of Rats edged in closer, whipping their tails and producing a strange grinding noise with their teeth. Queen Greenmould flinched and began to slump down in her basket as they pressed in tightly, staring deep into her eyes.

The Queen tried with all her might to resist. She heaved and puffed with the effort . . . but to no avail. Then, somewhere at the back of her mind, she remembered something . . . something she had heard about the nature of the Sacred Rats' strange, entrancing power.

'I know exactly what to do, Pulling Team,' she panted. 'Close your eyes tight. *Feel* your way forwards through the sludge. If you don't look, you won't be hypnotized. Do as I say, I order you – or we'll miss the Throne.'

In terror, the Pulling Team obeyed. Screwing their eyes up tight they took up the strain once more. The Queen's plan worked. The Contraption moved slowly forward, edging carefully along.

*

Underneath the throne, in a vaulted chamber below Westminster Abbey, Suzie heard the echo of Big Ben striking ten. It shuddered right down into her heart. In a few minutes' time she would have to escape, before the Queen tumbled through. She knew she had failed. She had tried *so hard* – but she had been thwarted at every turn. Deep inside she felt fully responsible for what her poor Queen was about to endure. It was *her* fault that the Sewer Creatures would all be caught and exterminated. She had let everybody down – as well as her own self. She wondered whether she would ever get over it. She would never be able to confess to anyone what had happened. She would have to keep it secret for the rest of her life. She sat down, put her head in her hands, and cried.

Up Above, a blast of trumpets greeted the arrival of the Queen's coach at Westminster. Her Majesty had arrived exactly on time at ten past ten. The Abbey was full to overflowing, its congregation listening to the organist's solemn music as bishops and archbishops took up their positions . . . and the final guest hurried to her place. Quickly the organist struck up the anthem, and the choir burst into an ecstasy of song as the Queen, in her royal robes, slowly and sedately progressed up the nave towards the throne.

Through a sewer tunnel that led to the chamber under the throne, a brave little Pig was squealing fit to burst in an effort to carry out his great mission. He felt, for once, properly important. He tried valiantly to egg Princess Griselda along, taking little nips at her ankles, or trying to push hard with his snout.

Under the throne, Suzie got up to flee.

Suddenly . . . a terrible wailing rent the sewer, as Princess Griselda hove into sight, Sir Pig Without Porkfolio close behind.

'My true fiancé is dead! Pompey ate him, and I loved him! How can I live without him? Oooh! Aaah!' she lamented, distraught.

'Of course – Princess Griselda! Just what we need! Well done, Pig, so *that's* where you've been! Stop, Princess Griselda, *stop*!' ordered Suzie, in a voice that had to be obeyed. 'Suppose I told you that your fiancé *hadn't* been eaten by Pompey, because I was there with him. What would you do?'

The Princess swerved to a halt.

'Anything. *Anything*,' she whimpered.

'Then, Griselda, you are about to perform the most *heroic* deed. Get hold of this chain and pull the Acro-prop upright.'

Grisely took the chain and pulled with all her might . . . But there was no response.

They heard the anthem swell up above. The Queen must be near her throne.

Suzie grew frantic. 'Princess Griselda, *really* pull!'

'I can't. I can't.'

'You can. You've *got* to!'

And the Princess did. She wrapped the chain around her body twice, so that the spare tyres took up the strain, and *threw* herself into it. Her eyes bulged. Spots stretched, then joined together in a seething sea of crimson. And as the organ gathered to its fullest force, thundering out, and as the choir of voices soared to its highest pitch, powerfully exalting . . . a strained, but familiar voice behind her croaked:

'Grisely, my Grisely!'

The Princess whirled round, to see Harold Foot-Webb being lugged along by the eight large Rats like a bundle of muddy old sewer-rags. With the chain still around her middle, Princess Griselda gave a tremendous *leap* towards him.

'*Squidgy*!' she yelped.

For an instant the prop shivered, then righted

itself . . . just as, Up Above, the Queen turned to sit on her throne.

'Well done, Grisely! You've done it! You've done it!' the little Pig squealed. The Grey Rats clapped profusely and danced around in a most unsacred way.

All at once, there was an unholy commotion as, from the opposite tunnel, the Contraption clattered in, pulled along by a hefty team of Rats, straining on their leashes. On its summit sat Queen Greenmould. Next to her was Lady Loo.

'Out of my way! Out of my way!' she shrieked, rattling her Sainsbury's trolley and thwacking the nearest Rats with her sceptre. 'I'm here to collect my booty. Where is it?' She pulled her team up short, so that a roadside grating fell off and a manhole cover tumbled away.

'You're *too late*, Mother!' proclaimed her daughter, proudly, all scarlet with delight and panting like a pump. 'The prop is upright, Her Majesty is saved – and I did it all myself.'

The Queen's mouth dropped open. For a moment or two there was silence while strains of the 'Vale Regina', sung by the choir Up Above, filtered down sounding like a strangled soprano, and the Grey Rats filed in procession to form a protective circle round the Acro, guarding and illuminating it as if it were a sacred relic. Then a gurgle like faulty plumbing issued from the back of the Queen's throat.

'Abominable child! You'll *pay* for this right *now*!' Whipping the Contraption Pulling Team into action, she ordered them to run her daughter over. But the eight large Rats had rushed forward gleefully, to fling themselves and their prisoner in front of the Queen in a tangled mass of mud, tails, spots and fur.

'We've come to claim our reward for capturing Ex-Prime Minister Foot-Webb. You promised five hundred buttons.'

The Queen's jowls collapsed and her brows contracted.

'What are *you* doing here, Prime Minister Foot-Webb? You're supposed to be dead. Pompey's eaten you.'

'No, you're drowned!' insisted Lady Loo. 'Sir Bounders Green told Lady Foulness, earlier today.'

'Well, you'd better die now – so things are straight. Kill him, Rats. No! Wait! First I want to find out what you did with my Alligator. Where is he?'

'He left your service,' said Suzie, stepping forward.

'You be quiet, One-Off. You've been eaten as well.'

'And drowned!' Lady Loo insisted.

'It was the Alligator's own decision to leave,' snorted the Pig.

'Swamp Pig! What are *you* doing here? You're meant to be trussed and ready to roast! You *will* be! And the rest of you shall die ... Rats, kill the lot of them!'

'*No!*' threatened Grisely, facing up to her mother.

'*Yes!*' roared the Queen, whirling her sceptre around.

'*No!*' growled a voice of great authority, behind.

And Igor the Rat stepped forward with heroic dignity.

He looked splendid. Instead of his red, white and blue bow tie, he now wore a line of war medals, which glinted spectacularly in the Grey Rats' flaming tapers. Behind him, scampering along the tunnel, was his own impressive 'Company of Rats'. At their front line strutted a terrifying group of great black rodents – warrior Rats, ready to bite. 'They must be the remains of the old English Ratocracy,' thought Suzie. They all had long, distinguished whiskers like Igor, and thwacked their tails hard on the ground. Behind them, Suzie saw a band of the fiercest, fattest creatures – every one as large as a cat. 'They must be the Gourmet Rats,' she gasped, 'from under the five-star hotels.' These looked as though they could suffocate you just by rolling on top of you. Every member of Igor's Company waited, alert and spoiling for action. Igor went straight up to the Queen and knocked her down.

'It's all over for you now, Greenmould,' he scowled, bristling his whiskers. 'And you're exactly where you should be. In the muck, down on your knees.' Then drawing himself up to full height, the Black Rat began to command. 'Release the Prime Minister!' he ordered the eight large Rats.

In front of Igor and his outfit the traitor Rats trembled and cringed.

'Yes, let him go!' gasped the Princess, with tears of relief welling from her eyes, like water oozing through a leaking bucket. 'He's mine!'

Snarling with disappointment the Rats were obliged to forfeit their prize. The exhausted Sludge-Gulper slumped forward – allowing Princess Griselda to race headlong, catch and enfold him in her arms, swamping him with kisses. It was far too slushy for Suzie to watch.

'Sludgey! Treasure of my heart,' he wept. 'So scarlet, so glistening, so damp.'

'Oh Squidgy!' she beamed, kissing him back like an air-lock.

Igor commanded the Pulling Team to be disbanded. The new Pulling Team would consist of the netted, squirming Greenback guards.

'You shan't get rid of me quite so easily,' rasped the Queen, shivering with emotion, so that pieces of sludge whirled away from her.

'You, Gulper Greenmould, will be retired, just like Her Majesty Up Above!'

The Queen's face contorted as Igor pronounced her sentence, and her spare tyres started to deflate. But the Rats dragged her to the Contraption, binding her to it tightly with Lady Loo's whip. She clung to the Sainsbury's trolley for support, and yelped as her hand was cut on the spokes of an old umbrella that formed part of the works.

Carefully, the exhausted Prime Minister was wrapped in the Union Jack and placed gently on a pile of post-office sacks in the Tesco trolley.

'Pull the Prime Minister back to the Palace,' growled Igor. 'Suzie and Princess Griselda can drive. Sir Pig Without Porkfolio shall lead the way. As for you, traitor Rats,' growled Igor, 'you can come with me and join the front line of fighting... and that goes for you too, Viscount Wapping and Baroness Squeaker-Brent. I and my Company of Rats mean to join the battle which is raging at this very moment underneath the Mall. From now on, I am in charge of every Rat in the Sewer. So follow me and look sharp!'

The trembling Rats crawled submissively to join the Company, their stomachs scraping low across the ground.

The Final Pong

Igor raced his Company of Rats at breakneck speed towards the incredible noise of the battle. He knew that the Queen's force had set out from the Palace – he intended to surprise them from the rear. Once every rodent was in place, Igor gave his command. Emitting a blood-curdling war-screech, the massive Rat-Pack scampered towards the rearguard of the Queen's army, plunging right into the fray, engaging the enemy in claw to claw combat.

Queen Greenmould's colossal army had been slowly gaining the upper hand, as wave after wave of its creatures kept surging forward to fight. Operation Royal Flush had almost run out of disinfectant, and they were on their final mops. But now, at the back of the Queen's army, the royal Rats whipped round, startled and confused. Was this new Rat force behind a friend or foe? Then one of them let out a piercing squeak. Wasn't that their old leader, Igor the Rat? Yes! There was his imposing form at the head of the Company, dressed in full military attire.

'Igor! Igor!' they screeched, and swarmed over to be at his side.

'The prop is in place,' he shrilled. 'Her Majesty Up Above is saved!'

More of the Queen's Rats, seeing his comeback, squealed with delight and ran to join him. Igor repositioned himself at the head of this enlarged Company of Rats, which now advanced with a whip of tails and a gnashing of teeth.

For several minutes there was chaos among the remaining Rats. Some turned on rodents they had fought alongside only seconds before, biting and scratching indiscriminately. Igor was calling something out again, as loud as he could. This new information – something about the Queen feeding her Alligator on Rats – whiffled fast through the remaining pockets of Rats. The news caused tremendous howls to erupt as they realized they had been deceived. They deserted in their dozens, raising their paws in surrender.

Operation Steamroller couldn't believe what was happening. Its commanders found themselves devoid of Rats, as well as being sandwiched uncomfortably between Igor's new force and the Sludge-Gulpers who, re-assembling fast, quickly lunged forward with a deafening croak, waving their final batch of mops. The Slime-Grubbers panicked, bunching close together. Many were trampled and squashed.

Lord Kenzal Green called wildly for help from the Honourable Harry Neasden, who had turned to confront the advancing Company of Rats. But this was now so swollen in number, that he swerved round again, preferring to fight the Sludge-Gulpers. With a piercing cry he urged his troops to make one last, great, savage attack.

Teeth and claws clashed with whirling disinfected mops, as the wretched Slime-Grubbers, snapping violently, tried to force a way through. Several of the fiercest bit clean through the mop-handles in their efforts. But the Sludge-Gulpers fought in a tight group, and behind the first line, there was a second one waiting.

Then suddenly Operation Royal Flush discovered there was no disinfectant left – or mops. In panic, Frogmorton called loudly to Shadwell and Chigwell for squeezer bottles of bleach to be rushed to the front. The next few assaults were made by Sludge-Gulpers leaping forward to overpower their victims with well-aimed jets of bleach, then crashing plastic buckets over their heads.

In howls of torment the Slime-Grubbers' mean eyes turned from yellow to red, while their green scaly skins whitened under the spray of volley after volley of bleach. They plunged about hope-lessly, frantic with pain. Fighting turned into struggling, then into humiliating defeat. One after another they yielded, putting up their claws in surrender. Before long it was all over. The enemy had given in.

'We got 'em. We got 'em!' screamed Edna Pongworthy, triumphant in the front line of bleach.

'We've won!' cheered Rickmansworthy and Purley from another quarter.

'Forward with the captives! Storm the Palace!' cried Chigwell and Angel Rat from somewhere else.

Keeping the prisoners sandwiched in their midst, Igor turned and led them victoriously towards the Palace, with the Sludge-Gulpers marching on behind. When they stormed the entrance, they found the place almost empty. Lady Foulness was forced to let them in.

Not far behind the victors, a weird procession, led by the flaming tapers from the entire Sacred Company of Grey Rats, followed the wider sewer under Whitehall to trundle its way back to the Palace. Prime Minister Harold Foot-Webb had requested Ignatius to accompany them in order to perform a Sacred Ceremony of Marriage between himself and Princess Griselda. The whole of the sacred sect had been invited to celebrate, too, in return for the vital part they had played in saving the Throne. Ignatius had kindly agreed. But first they had laid out the small Grey Rat that Queen Greenmould had killed so cruelly, planting lighted tapers around it in the mud, and chanting the last rites over it. Then, after some difficulty, the netted Slime-Grubbers had been harnessed unwillingly to haul the Contraption.

Ex-Queen Greenmould was made to trudge through the sludge, tied to one corner of the Sainsbury's trolley with Lady Loo's whip. She was fuming so much, that foam dribbled from the folds of her munching jowls. Lady Loo was fastened to the trolley from Tesco, and stumbled along complaining bitterly. The Slime-Grubbers at the back of the Pulling Team kept turning to sneer at the prisoners, and kicked up at them with scratchy back claws.

'It's your fault we've been overcome!' they jabbered.

Suzie and Princess Griselda sat on top of the Contraption, clinging on as best they could, attempting to drive. Harold Foot-Webb slowly recovered, snugly wrapped in the Union Jack on a pile of sacks. The Little Pig trotted beside Ignatius, carrying Ex-Queen Greenmould's crown in his snout. A further contingent of Grey Rats lit the procession from behind.

Up Above, the long Abdication Ceremony had come to an end. The Ex-Queen left Westminster Abbey, the bells ringing out. Crowds waved flags and cheered 'Farewell' as, minus her crown, sceptre and orb, she climbed into her golden coach for the return journey.

Down Below, Sludge-Gulper Greenmould started to unpick one or two of the old shoelaces which made up Lady Loo's whip, gradually loosing herself from the Contraption. Then she extracted the remains of the old umbrella from the body-work, pretending to use it to help herself along. She kept her eyes fixed on the roof overhead.

Under Trafalgar Square they rattled, and into the High Interceptory Level Sewer under the Mall, where the Contraption lurched over bits of broken mop-handle, split plastic buckets, crushed bottles of bleach, and other signs of war.

*

Up Above, the Royal procession clattered along Whitehall and swung into Trafalgar Square. It went round the fountains before wheeling through Admiralty Arch to sweep up the Mall, flashing past geraniums and salvias which hung from lamp-posts in brightly coloured baskets. The crowds cheered it along with a deafening roar.

Meanwhile, Down Below, the Contraption had just reached the end of the Mall when, at a particular place which Greenmould knew well, an umbrella suddenly jammed the spokes of a pram wheel under the Contraption, jerking it to a halt. While Suzie and Princess Griselda got down to inspect the spokes, the Queen broke free of her binding and scrambled on to the Sainsbury's trolley. By balancing on this, she could just reach up to a manhole cover, positioned exactly above her head. She started pushing it open with her large webbed hands.

'Don't let her escape!' yelled Princess Griselda.

'Don't go without *me*!' pleaded Water Loo, clinging to a webbed foot above her. But the Queen trod down hard on her companion's head.

'Your services are no longer required, thank you, Loo.'

239

'She mustn't go Up Above, or she'll be *seen*!' cried Harold Foot-Webb, frantically trying to unroll himself from the flag.

In front of them, the Sacred Rats had stopped and turned back with their tapers. All at once, the Swamp Pig saw what to do. He scrambled on to the Contraption to bite at Greenmould's ankle. But, as his teeth sank in, they had the wrong effect, for she gave a great yelp and shot easily upwards out of the manhole, and slammed the cover firmly down behind . . .

She was not seen at all Up Above. All eyes were turned to catch a last glimpse of the Ex-Queen through the window of her golden coach as it bowled down the centre of the Mall. The crowds were cheering 'Goodbye' hysterically.

The heavy State coach rolled straight over Ex-Queen Greenmould with a wet *splat*!

The coach hardly lurched at all, but rattled onwards to leave the brown explosion to be trodden over . . . by first the Household Cavalry; next, the Grenadier Guards; next, the Coldstream Guards; next, the Scots Guards, the Irish Guards, and finally the Welsh Guards. But all of them were hit by an appalling pong as if from a thousand sewers, and they began to sneeze and veer slightly out of line. By the time the bevy of Beefeaters had marched on by, there was only the faintest smudge of sludge, spread liberally over the route. And when the cheering crowd closed in behind them, the remains of Ex-Queen Greenmould were dispersed underfoot in smaller and smaller stains for ever.

CHAPTER TWENTY-FIVE

The Coronation

Having circled the gushing blue fountain in front of the Palace, the golden coach rattled finally through the gilded wrought-iron gates into the courtyard. Outside, the crowd surged together in a great sea of faces, turning upwards to the balcony, to watch for the Queen's farewell wave. As the Queen climbed from her coach, she sighed. What a wonderful goodbye her people had given her, and what a happy retirement lay ahead in the country up in Sandringham. Her corgis waddled out to meet her. They, too, looked happy and healthy . . . except for some strange green stains around their snouts.

'What have you been up to, scallywags?' she asked, leaning forward to pat them. The corgis backed away from the coach. There was a horrid smell coming from the wheels that they didn't like. The Queen wrinkled her nose, too, as she entered her Palace for the final time.

Down Below, a terrible pong filtered from the manhole above the Contraption. It became obvious that Ex-Queen Greenmould had been squashed.

'The tyrant is dead,' they called. Relief swept through the procession which, choking on the smell, said no more but continued on to the Sewer Palace at a faster pace.

Cheering greeted them on their arrival. Their victorious army rushed from the Palace in welcome, happy to see their former leaders alive.

'We've had a glorious fight!' called Purley. 'But, by Bazalgette, I'm glad it's all over and you're still with us.'

Stories were swapped, and everybody was more than thankful to hear of their deliverance from the dreadful Queen, and delighted with the help the Grey Rats had given. They crowded into the Throne Room to enjoy the celebrations of a thousand fairy lights and masses of bubbling champagne.

Princess Griselda left her friends for a while. She returned radiant and fitting perfectly into her pearly wedding gown – for she had lost more than enough weight by pulling up the prop.

Harold Foot-Webb could wait no longer to be married, and insisted on speed. But just as the wedding ceremony was about to begin, there was a stirring in the mud next to the fountain, and King Gropius revived from his stupor suffering a terrible hangover. He opened bleary eyes, and sang, 'Guinness is good for you', as he staggered to his feet, in time to give his daughter away. 'Ehem! It's the second suitor got you I see.'

When the King was told of his Queen's foul end, he looked as if a great weight had lifted from his mind and a great burden from his side.

The bride flushed shyly to a delicate pink as Ignatius attempted to join their webbed hands in matrimony, but they kept on slipping apart. Eventually he entwined their hands in a love knot with his tail to hold them tight in place until the vows were finalized.

'Oh Squidgy!' swooned the Princess, her eyes two whirlpools of delight.

'Oh Sludgey!' called Harold Foot-Webb, clenching her in a muddy embrace.

'Hurrah! Hurrah!' cheered the court.

'C'mon Lady Foulness,' ordered King Gropius, 'we'd better fetch more Abdication Champagne to congratulate the happy bride and groom, eh what?'

Then Harold Foot-Webb raised his hand to

silence the crowd, and stood on the Root to speak.

'Which would you prefer Under London, my brave Sludge-Gulpers and Loyal Rats, a Republic or a Monarchy?'

'Long live Queen Griselda and King Harold Foot-Webb!' someone called.

Immediately the cry was taken up and echoed around.

'We *will* be King and Queen,' said Harold Foot-Webb, 'but Parliament must decide all laws.'

'And everyone must be allowed to vote,' added Princess Griselda. 'I would like to propose Purley and Edna as joint Pearly Prime Ministers, if everyone agrees?'

Everyone did – unanimously.

As the Royal Pair sat down on their Roots to be crowned, Suzie walked up slowly to drape the Union Jack around Harold Foot-Webb for his coronation cloak. The maintenance man's mac fitted Griselda perfectly for hers.

Sir Pig Without Porkfolio passed the crown of bits and pieces to Frogmorton, who presented it to Ignatius, who, with the utmost ceremony, set it on Harold Foot-Webb's head.

'Long live our new King!' they all cried. Then there was an awkward pause, and everyone looked embarrassed. Where was the crown for Queen Griselda?

But Suzie had thought of that. She still wore round her head the maintenance man's sewer torch. Deftly she unstrapped the band.

'Princess Griselda, here is your wedding present. It's a very special type of crown.'

'Oh scrumptious! Put it on, quick!' The Princess's voice rose an octave with excitement as Suzie adjusted it to her size, then instructed Ignatius to switch it on. Solemnly Ignatius obliged.

At once the Sewer Crown beamed powerfully out.

'Oooh!' went the admiring crowd as it shot a silver circle round the room. 'Queen Griselda!' they cheered, as with the sceptre set in her hand, she was crowned by Ignatius.

'Long live Queen Griselda! Long live King Harold Foot-Webb!' they chanted . . . until King Harold Foot-Webb rose to quieten them. And his voice had grown very serious, so everyone was still.

'Today, we have avoided a terrible disaster, thanks to the bravery of you all. But we have also learned that sometimes the old ways turn out to be best. So, from now on I propose we return to the way of life we had before: Sludge-Gulpers gulping sludge, Slime-Grubbers grubbing walls, Rats eating anything else. No one will own any land – and once again our sewers will be free.'

'And what about that disgraceful Lady Loo?' called Rickmansworthy.

'Water Loo, you mean,' Shadwell growled.

'*I've* been thinking about that,' said Jacusi, stepping forward. 'She deserves something very tedious and dull as she's behaved so atrociously. Send her to be chained up under a prison – somewhere like Wormwood Scrubs – and let her be grateful for whatever comes down.'

'Oogh, you wouldn't!' gulped Water Loo, her eyes stretching like flexible piping.

'Good thinking,' chuckled Chigwell. 'High time she met her Waterloo. Ha!'

Water Loo stood up, shaking and trembling. She pointed at Suzie.

'It's *you*, stupid One-Off, who's responsible for all this turmoil!'

'Yes, thank you, Suzie, you are,' said Queen Griselda. 'And thank you, Swamp Pig and everyone else who helped. Suzie shall have the highest position in my Court, with Edna. Down on your knees, please . . . Arise Lady Edna Pongworthy. Arise Lady Suzie One-Off.' And she hit them on their shoulders with her mother's sceptre.

'Please,' asked Suzie, 'now everything has

come right, may I go back home? – and I'm very pleased about my title,' she added quickly.

'Could I ask for something, too?' squealed the Pig. 'Can I go with her?'

Suzie was delighted. She had grown very attached to the Swamp Pig.

Further champagne was poured, and there was an awful lot of slime involved in the shaking of hands during the farewells.

Meanwhile, a group set off for the Sauna Baths where the injured had been taken. They would tell Flotsam, Jetsam and the infant Gulpers the good news, and take champagne for Granny and Grandad Gulper. Also it was suggested to Gropius that maybe, in a few days' time, he should stay for a time up a Dry Riser Outlet, until he was less of an old soak.

Lady Suzie One-Off felt quite light-headed when she and the Swamp Pig finally left on their journey back. The Sacred Rats re-lit their tapers one after the other from Gropius's methane gas lighter, and prepared to head the procession back to Suzie's home. And it was marvellous to travel in complete safety through the London Sewers. From every grating, a muffled peal of bells filtered down, becoming fainter and fainter as they neared her home.

Queen Griselda and King Harold Foot-Webb

escorted Suzie to the lift, their eyes brimming with tears as Suzie said goodbye to everyone.

'Good luck, dearest Lady One-Off. Thank you for everything.'

'Farewell,' said the Sacred Company of Rats.

'Because the Acro-prop is in my sacred territory,' said Ignatius, 'I promise to ensure that it always stays in place.'

CHAPTER TWENTY-SIX

Fireworks

The people of London cheered farewell to their Queen until they were hoarse. Then they looked forward to tea and a rest before returning to watch the firework display and laser show. Lines of friends filled the streets linking arms, or talked together quietly in groups until, melting into an outward-flowing crowd, they dispersed homewards. For once there was no traffic – only a full peal of bells ringing out. It was wonderful.

The service lift ground its way to the eighteenth floor of Suzie's block. Suzie had grown increasingly hot and thirsty as her procession had made its way towards Pimlico. Now, with the little Pig snuffling close to her feet, it was as if she was floating. She felt strangely distant from the trouble she was expecting. When the lift lurched to a halt, she stepped from it like an automaton.

They were all there, waiting, both inside and outside the flat: Jane, with a tear-stained face; Clare, looking pale; Clare's parents, Mr and Mrs Hainault; Jane's mother; Suzie's own mother – even Uncle Ongar. And they looked so agitated that the Pig held back nervously in the shadows.

When they saw Suzie come towards them safe and well, all of them broke into fresh floods of tears. Suzie's mother gave a cry and rushed to her daughter. She flung her arms around her – but only briefly, because of the smell.

'Darling,' she cried. 'Where were you? We've all been *so* worried. When I got back from work, you weren't there! What have you been doing? Are you all right?'

The door was closing, when a little muddy pig whiffled through it, dashed past, and disappeared under the sofa.

'Oh!' screamed Mrs Stanmore, jumping on to the sofa.

'I'm sorry, Mummy, I wanted to watch the procession live, from a place by the side of the Mall. Then I saw this pig, trapped down a grating. I had to rescue him . . .'

'First a kitten "rescue", next a pig "rescue" . . . Oh darling, really!'

'But I *have* to *keep* him, Mummy, as a pet. I

can, can't I? He doesn't belong to anybody – he's got nowhere to go.'

'No, darling, not really ... not a pig,' Mrs Southgate gasped. 'I'm sorry, but definitely not. Whoever heard of a pig living eighteen storeys up?'

'The child obviously needs a pet of some sort,' said Mrs Hainault. 'I think all this trouble has been about that.'

After a lot of debate, Uncle Ongar came up with a solution. He explained how, whilst working on a shop near to Suzie's school, he had to travel past the City Farm in Vauxhall. Couldn't the little pig go to the City Farm? It would have lots of other pigs there for company.

'And I believe they're needing people to help look after the animals. Why don't you three girls help on the farm at weekends? Then you can still see your pig.'

'We could take our whole class to see him one day, couldn't we?' said Clare, eagerly.

'Would you really let me help as well?' asked Jane, rather quietly. 'I'm sorry if I've been unfriendly to you. You can play with my kitten whenever you want. And I promise to do your maths – without any Smarties—'

'No you won't,' Jane's mother corrected. 'You'll teach Suzie *how* to do maths, explain things – not do it *for* her – won't you, Jane?'

252

'Yes, I will, I will . . .'

So it was decided that Uncle Ongar would take the little pig to the City Farm on his way home. There was bound to be someone there to attend to him. And it transpired that Uncle Ongar had only happened to drop in to see them because he was taking a spare Acro-prop along to the shop he was doing up. There had been reports that one had been stolen from there, and the ceiling had nearly come down.

'The missing prop will be covered by my insurance, though, so everything will be all right.'

Suzie smiled and nodded as she scratched the Pig behind his ears. 'I wish I could tell him that his missing Acro is now the most important prop in the country, holding up the throne,' she thought.

Mrs Stanmore rang the police to tell them of her daughter's safe return, then they all sat down for their Abdication tea. Afterwards, Suzie picked up the Pig from where he had fallen fast asleep in front of the gas fire, and placed him in the safety of her uncle's arms. She trusted Uncle Ongar completely.

'Goodbye Swamp Pig, for now,' she whispered.

Clare's mother, standing next to her, heard her

muttering. She placed a hand on Suzie's flushed forehead.

'Goodness!' she exclaimed. 'The child's boiling hot! She must be running a fever.'

'It's bathtime and bed for you, straight away,' her mother pronounced. She ran Suzie a bath.

After everyone had left, Suzie soaked in the hot bath. When she came out, she found her mother slumped exhausted in front of the telly, watching the Abdication ceremony on video. Suzie felt guilty. Her mother hadn't been able to enjoy the ceremony at all, and she must have been worried almost out of her mind. She snuggled next to her on the sofa, wrapped in her dressing gown.

Suzie's favourite bit was when the Queen sat down on her throne to give up her crown to the Archbishop of Canterbury. There was an anxious moment when it looked as though the throne shifted ever so slightly . . . but it could have been camera shake. Over the Queen's face came a fleeting look of panic – though she quickly composed herself.

'One must never jump up and down on the marble squares next to the throne in the Abbey,' Suzie warned quietly.

Her mother looked at her. 'You're not feeling at all well, are you, poor thing? I'll get you a nice mug of chocolate, and if you fall asleep watching, I can carry you to bed. You won't miss anything. The video will be here tomorrow.'

She came back with two steaming drinks inside two Abdication mugs from work. Neither of them felt like eating.

When the first rocket whizzed up over the Serpentine and burst into a shower of silver spangles high in the sky, they stopped the video and sat near the window to watch.

'I've made lots of money painting Abdication mugs,' her mother said. 'How about going down to Brighton for the next three days, to rest and get some fresh air? Monday is a bank holiday after all. What do you think?'

Suzie's answer was rather strange: 'The Brighton Sewerage stretches back ever so far . . . They'll bathe in the Albion Overflow.' And she sang softly:

'There'll be little bits of fish and chips With plenty of salt by the sea.

'. . . and King Harold Foot-Webb and Queen Griselda on their Brighton honeymoon will be ever so delighted to know that Lady Suzie One-Off will be holidaying directly Up Above . . .'

'What, darling?' Mrs Southgate felt Suzie's brow again. 'Perhaps I'd better take your temperature – you're saying such strange things.'

Suzie was given two aspirins and tucked into bed. Her mother sat beside her, soothing her brow until she fell into a deep, relaxing sleep.

'It'll take both of us a while to get used to this new way of life,' she thought. 'But I'll try to make it a better one – be with her more, go on excursions, do exciting things . . . I'll have to try being both mother and father to her now.'

Mrs Southgate lowered her head to avoid the strange lights flickering from the sky outside. Piercing laser beams seemed to be flashing from every high building in town. Sharp lines of bright colour danced frantically around the bedroom wall, mesmerizing her with green dots and spots of day-glo pink.

Mrs Southgate rested her head on her daughter's pillow. Then she fell fast asleep.

Suzie dreamed that down below Buckingham Palace, King Harold Foot-Webb was sitting next to Queen Griselda, who clutched a freshly cleaned blue sceptre, while the Sewer Crown beamed powerfully from her brow. Together they ruled from their Throne Roots over the Sewers of London. She turned over, hot and feverish, and dreamed of an Alligator swimming out towards the cool Thames Estuary, and imagined him reaching the wide open sea . . .

Also by Jane Waller
Saving the Dinosaurs

At first, finding you've been sent the wrong computer disk by mistake is plain inconvenient.

All too soon, it turns out to be a passport to an undiscovered world – lost in the depths of time . . .

Will Peter ever return from the Late Cretaceous Age? Once back, will he be able to save his new-found friends from certain doom? And how long will it take the *other* Peter Phillips to catch up with him?

Eva Ibbotson
The Secret of Platform 13

Under Platform 13 at King's Cross Station there is a gump. Few people know that gumps are doors leading to other worlds. And this one opens for exactly nine days every nine years.

On the other side is a hand-picked team on a daring rescue mission. Odge Gribble, a young hag, together with an invisible ogre, a doddery wizard, a magical fey and an enchanted mistmaker, must bring back the Prince of their kingdom, stolen as a baby nine years before.

But the Prince has become a horrible boy called Raymond Trottle, who is determined not to be rescued . . .